LOVE LIKE FIRE

Hearts in Hendricks Book Two

D.E. MALONE

LOVE LIKE FIRE

For information, contact dawnemalone@gmail.com
Love Like Fire
Copyright © 2018 D.E. Malone
All rights reserved.
ISBN (paperback) 978-0-9903242-6-3
(ebook) 978-0-9903242-7-0
Cover designed by Seedlings Design Studio
First Edition

Subscribe to D.E. Malone's newsletter by visiting www.demalone.com

SUMMARY: Not one for commitments, Bethany Marconi struggles with her self-imposed dating rules when long-time admirer Nate Ransom returns to Hendricks to settle his grandmother's estate.

Also by D.E. Malone

Love Like Water #1

Love Like Fire #2

Love Like Air #3

Love Like Forever #4

Love, Lies and Fireflies, a Blueberry Point Story

Love, Lies and Lavender #1

Love, Lies and Mistletoe #2

Love, Lies and Lullabies #3

Love, Lies and Lemon Pie #4

A Forever Kiss in Silver Leaf Falls

Writing Middle Grade as Dawn Malone

The Upside of Down

Bingo Summer

For the latest book happenings, special subscriber giveaways, and advance notice on sales and new releases, please subscribe to D.E. Malone's newsletter by visiting her website.

One spark ignites
From words or a wink,
Hope weaving its golden thread
Through a forest overgrown
With ire, lies and fear.
For it seeks, smoldering and emboldened
By the wish for more tender kindling,
The source of its heart's desire —
Love.

— *Silas Penn*

Chapter One

Bethany Marconi opened one eye and studied her phone on the futon's arm across the living room. It buzzed like a swarm of bees for the second time within the minute, its vibration moving the device across the arm until it fell onto the cushion. Whoever it was needed a lesson in patience.

Legs crossed, shoulders back, she closed her eye to continue with the breathing exercise as the phone grew quiet.

In…out…eleven…

Again, the incessant buzzing interrupted the silence.

In…out…twelve…

Bethany opened her eyes and glared at the phone.

"Seriously?"

She relaxed her torso, shook out her legs, and crawled off her yoga mat to the couch. Darcy's name was on the screen.

Bethany balanced the phone between her ear and shoulder as she stood. "Hello?"

"We just had our first fight," her best friend said on the other end. "I need to talk. I'm going crazy."

"I wondered when that would happen. You lovebirds were due." Bethany rolled the mat up and stuffed it behind the futon.

"Are you busy?" Darcy asked. Her husky voice was an octave higher than usual.

Bethany slipped her jacket off the coat tree, grabbed her wallet and keys, and opened the door. "Not anymore. Meet you at Debi's in ten minutes. Scone and coffee are on me."

If there was one thing Bethany was good at, it was matchmaking. Never mind the number of blind dates which had gone up in flames—she wasn't *that* good. What mattered were the couples who stayed together, the ones who overcame the pitfalls after the honeymoon months wore off and before the engagement announcement. Bethany counted four weddings to date, all credited to her. That was why she was out the door in minutes when Darcy called in dire need of a shoulder to cry on. Darcy and Sean Stetman would be the fifth wedding. Someday. As soon as Stetman got his act together and proposed.

Five minutes later, Bethany wheeled into the first parking space in front of Debi's Donuts, a diminutive place with pink siding and gingerbread trim. Beyond the building, Lake Superior reflected the clear January sky, a liquid sheet of cerulean glass. The colors were a beautiful contrast, and when Bethany stepped out of her car, she took a moment to breathe deeply and revel in the scenery.

She'd console and listen. She'd let Darcy talk for what, five minutes, maybe? Then and only then would Bethany open her mouth. Improving her listening skills was her New Year's resolution. She'd been doing fairly well, given that she'd been at it a solid week. It was part of her living mindfully project, and admittedly, it was *hard*.

Darcy's Jeep pulled in behind her. Even through the windshield, Bethany could tell Darcy was upset. Her raven curls, usually loose around her shoulders, were tamed in a headband, which wouldn't be a telltale sign of her mood necessarily, but with her hair swept off her face, the angry slashes of her eyebrows were on full display.

Bethany opened Darcy's car door and stood aside as her friend struggled to get out of the driver's seat without unfastening her belt. She watched Darcy strain against it for a few seconds, growing more and more upset. Finally and without a word, Bethany reached over Darcy and released the belt.

"You need to breathe, friend. Everything'll be fine."

Darcy gave her a sheepish look. "I doubt it. It was bad," she said, stepping out of the car. She reached inside to grab her bag from the passenger seat, only the bag's handle wrapped around the shift lever when she pulled on it, yanking her back onto the seat.

Darcy groaned and pounded the steering wheel. The horn emitted an abrupt honk, startling two ravens resting on the pitched roof of the donut shop. She jerked her bag out of the car and slammed the door.

"If one more thing doesn't go right today, I'm seriously going to empty my bank account and run away."

"I don't think I've ever seen you this mad."

Darcy shook her head, slinging her bag over one shoulder. "This is nothing. You should have seen me after I got off the phone with Sean."

Bethany opened the door for Darcy, and the two walked into the euphoria of sweetness. Debi's place brought about an instant calm, though Bethany wondered if anything could soothe Darcy at the moment. She opened her wallet and pointed to the window seat.

"Go sit down. The usual?"

Darcy sighed. "Yes, please, though no coffee. That would just fuel my ranting."

"Maybe you need to rant. Better to me than to Sean."

A few minutes later, Bethany brought the warm scones cradled in their napkins to where Darcy waited, drumming her fingers on the tabletop.

Bethany slid into the vinyl booth. "Okay. Spill it."

Darcy's shoulders slumped as she relaxed against the back of the booth. She stuck a stirrer into her coffee mug. "Sean has been under a lot of stress—making repairs at the lodge and driving the tours. He doesn't have much downtime."

"Yes, you've mentioned that."

Darcy looked out the window toward the water. "Well, I told him that I was going to Marquette for a long weekend to see Mom. I'm taking Friday off since we don't have a tour booked," she said, glancing at Bethany before she continued stirring her coffee absentmindedly.

"Go on." Bethany guessed where this was heading,

wanted to ask if she was right, but her silent pledge was still only seconds old. *Keep it zipped.*

"I casually asked if he wanted to come with, you know, so he wouldn't feel left out of my plans. And he totally snapped." Darcy threw up her hands. "I was only thinking of him, yet he accused me of asking him to drop everything and take off."

Bethany nodded knowingly. Yes, she knew exactly the trigger in that scenario. Old flames die hard.

"The Ghost of Paige." So much for listening.

Darcy nodded. "You got it. He didn't mention her by name, but I did, and that was my mistake. But being compared to her drives me crazy. Completely nuts! Or the *thought* of the comparison, that is."

Bethany brushed the crumbs off her pants. "What did you say exactly?"

Darcy gritted her teeth. "You know my problem with not being able to filter words, right?"

"Just tell me. Maybe it's not as bad as you think."

She groaned. "I said if he's still stuck on what happened in the past, maybe he's not ready for a future with me."

"Harsh but true."

Darcy shrank farther into the booth. "That's not all."

"Uh-oh."

"Yeah." Darcy swirled the stir stick a few more times. "I said that I didn't want him to go after all because he clearly loves his job more than me." She looked at Bethany. "I said no wonder Paige dumped him."

It was Bethany's turn to cringe. "Yikes. You told him that?"

"Yes."

"And how did you guys end the conversation?"

"I hung up on him."

"Ouch. You don't mess around." Bethany grabbed the stick out of Darcy's cup, ending the maddening repetition of stick stirring. "Well, you'll just have to call him back and work through it."

"I knew you'd say that."

"What other solution is there? You were mean. He was too. It won't get better by ignoring it."

"I know. That's what mature couples do, right? Apologize? Talk it out?"

Bethany wanted to say that she didn't really know from personal experience, but yes, that usually happened in every romance novel she read. Whoever screws up apologizes and changes into a new, improved version of himself or herself if the couple has any chance of staying together. Apart from her romantic literary expertise, Bethany never got to the point in a relationship to apologize. The first fight was typically the last fight. Then she'd cut her new ex-boyfriend loose to lick his wounds and wonder what natural disaster occurred to upend his love life so completely. Romantic bliss and Bethany were not synonymous.

"What if he's not okay with my apology?" Darcy's eyebrows dipped as she looked away. The firm set of her mouth told Bethany that her friend worried about the worst-case scenario.

"Darcy, don't be ridiculous. Sean loves you."

Darcy chewed on her lip, shaking her head slightly.

"What, you doubt that? C'mon, seriously? He'd be the

ground you walk on if it were physically possible. He worships you."

"I know he does." Darcy sighed. "He's been working so hard, too, and I had to use that against him. I feel rotten."

"We all are on occasion."

"You never have problems like this. What's your secret?"

"When was the last time I dated someone longer than a couple months?"

Darcy gave her a deadpan look.

Bethany held her finger up. "That's my secret."

They laughed together, and Bethany could tell the joke eased some of Darcy's tension, because she finally took a bite of her scone.

"Why is that, Bethany? Seriously. You're never lacking for dates. A lot of them are nice guys, too, from what I can tell."

Crossing her arms over her chest, Bethany gazed out the window. She'd just as soon look inward as she would keep a steady boyfriend. If she thought deep enough, the reasons usually turned toward her career-obsessed parents, and Gran, who essentially raised her, and those were thoughts for another day.

"I just don't like to be tied down, I guess. Too much to do without lovey-dovey stuff to tend to."

Darcy smiled. "You're funny." Darcy's look lingered on Bethany. "I like your hair, by the way. What'd you do to it?"

Bethany shrugged and fluffed one side. "Cropped it a little shorter. Got it lightened. I'm still not used to having nothing below my shoulders."

"I love it. It suits you."

"Thanks. I think winter was the wrong time to go shorter though. I think my neck has frostbite."

Darcy laughed. After a moment, the smile faded from Darcy's face. "There's something else that has been kind of bothering me too."

"What's that?"

"Funny you brought up the Ghost of Paige, because she's not going to be just a memory soon." Darcy nodded when Bethany's mouth popped open. "Yeah, she's *baaack,*" Darcy squealed.

"What for?"

"She was assigned a photo feature of the North Shore for some travel magazine. Since we expanded with the lodge, she'll be doing a side article on Sturgeon Widows Tours."

"Did she call you?"

"She called the company, and Sean happened to answer. He mentioned her calling but didn't want to say much more about it. I think he's mad more than anything—mad that he'll have to put up with her off and on for a couple weeks or so."

"You could be the contact person for her. Wouldn't that be a hoot?"

Darcy laughed. "Don't think I didn't consider it."

Bethany sipped her coffee. "Well, let me know if you need me. First fight aside, there's nothing that would make me more giddy than a happily-ever-after for you two. And anything—or anyone—who gets in the way...well, watch out."

"I know. Thanks for listening," Darcy said. She patted the top of Bethany's hand. "That reminds me. Tickets go on sale this week for the Red Hot Gala. It's the weekend before Valentine's Day. I have two with your name on it. Consider this a call to action to find a date."

Bethany rubbed her hands together. "I'll have to think about the timing carefully. If I find someone too soon, there's the chance he won't be in the picture come February."

"True. And you won't want to miss our inaugural gala at Blueberry Point Lodge. It's going to be magical."

"With you in charge, I don't doubt it."

Darcy drained her mug. "I should get to work. Hopefully I can catch Sean without his mother or Melina there." She slid out of the booth and hugged Bethany. "Thanks again. You're always the voice of reason."

Bethany laughed. "I think you're exaggerating. I'm just a good listener. But thanks."

Darcy left with a bounce in her step, and Bethany smiled to herself while she wiped the table free of crumbs and finished the last swallow of coffee. It had taken forever to get those two together, even though Bethany knew they'd be perfect for each other. They'd only been dating four months, a time when those little insecurities start to creep in and upend everything. But she wouldn't know that from personal experience. No way. And Bethany wouldn't find out any time soon either if it was up to her.

Chapter Two

N ate Ransom sat on the edge of the coffee table in his late grandmother's parlor, bent over a box of photos. The late-afternoon sun poured through the window blinds, casting tiger stripes onto the carpet and the watercolor canvases, large and small, leaning against the far wall. He'd been packing her artwork since lunch, gifts from her artist friends over the years. But the decoupaged box of photos stashed onto the topmost shelf of her hutch caught his eye.

Curl-edged and yellowing, the images captivated him. So many memories. So many laughs. He chuckled aloud, drawing an irritated look from his younger sister, Jana.

Nate waved a photo at her.

"Look at this one. Remember the story behind the canoe? The piece of junk almost killed me."

Jana crossed the room, brushing her hands against the sides of her sweatshirt, and peered at the photo. "What I remember might be a different version of what you remember. Dad blamed you for paddling us into that giant tree limb that had fallen across the river."

Nate shook his head. "Not my fault. That was my first solo ride without Dad. I wasn't ready to command my own canoe."

His sister shoved him playfully in the shoulder. "Please. You were more than ready, Mr. Boy Scout," Jana said, taking the photo out of his hand and dropping it back into the box. "Now we have work to do if we're going to be ready for the auction."

Nate shuffled through another handful of photos, bringing them closer to see the details. Taking a trip down memory lane hadn't been in the plans, but he couldn't help it. A few more minutes of reminiscing wouldn't hurt anything.

Outside, the wind howled against the house even though it was five blocks from the lake and buffered by a row of arborvitae to the north. The sun waned behind a thick bank of clouds, darkening the room for a moment. Nate looked toward the window, watching the tree branches sway against each other.

The room was heavy on dark, imposing furniture, and the thick, shag rug the color of mustard didn't do much to lighten its mood. The first thing Jana had done when they'd opened up the house last week was throw back the drapes and let some light inside the rooms. He wished his break between writing assignments had fallen during a month with better weather. Visiting Hendricks in the midst of its notoriously brutal winter was bad timing on his part. And of course, Mom had scheduled the auction for the week after she and Dad were due to return home from their winter place in Phoenix. So preparing the house had fallen to him and his sister.

Jana looked over his shoulder at another photo he'd found. The picture was of him and Jana, two towheaded kids, standing next to the playhouse his grandfather had built in the backyard.

"Funny, it seems so much smaller than I remember it." She tucked her hair behind one ear. "Gosh, look how skinny you were."

Nate stood and rubbed his stomach. "Yeah, yeah. Don't rub it in."

She handed the photo back to him. "You're so sensitive. That's not what I meant."

"I can't help that I've stopped growing up and started growing out."

Jana looked him up and down. "Please. You could put on a ton and still attract females like flies to jelly."

"Yes, people would definitely look at me if I gained two thousand pounds."

She laughed. "You know what I mean. Have you forgotten how I used to complain to Mom that my friends were more interested in seeing you when they came over than hanging out with me?"

"They just liked me because I made them laugh. And because I'd give them all plastic rings on their birthdays."

"Yes! Those plastic rings of yours." Jana chuckled. "You were so smooth."

Nate dropped the photo into the box and brushed his knuckles against the pockets of his shirt. "Still am."

"Please," she said, laughing.

Jana carried the box to the farthest corner of the room, away from Nate because his sister knew him well enough. That box was a big distraction. Four years younger, Jana acted like his mother at times, simultaneously irritating him and making him thankful someone could rein in his impulses and procrastination. Maybe it was her experience in a fifth-grade classroom, commanding twenty 10- and 11-year-olds for seven hours five days a week. That took some mettle and an art for distraction, he figured.

Jana snapped her fingers. "That reminds me. Remember that girl you crushed on all throughout school? What was her name?"

Nate raked his hand through his hair. "How could I forget? Bethany Marconi."

Jana pointed at him. "Yes! That's it."

"I ran out of those plastic rings before I could give her one in third grade. She hated me for that up until we moved away."

"I don't blame her."

"I didn't realize the power of those rings. So? What about her?"

"I saw her today. She has her own yoga studio downtown."

"Really? I figured everyone I knew back then moved away."

"Nope. A few people have stuck around. I'm having coffee with Kelley Martin tomorrow. Remember her? Waist-long braids? She used to get picked for the kickball teams during recess before most of the boys."

"How could I forget? I might have been one of those boys a time or two."

Jana chuckled. "She's still here, doing the accounting for her dad's heating and air conditioning place." Jana pulled out the top drawer of an antique cabinet and brought it over for Nate to sort. "Anyway, I thought you'd be interested to know that your grade school infatuation is within walking distance in case, you know, you want to make up for that plastic ring debacle."

Nate pushed around the contents of the drawer. "You know, I might have to take you up on that." He distinctly remembered Bethany's white-blonde hair and how hard she used to slug him in the arm when he got caught staring at her too long. Nate rubbed his arm absentmindedly. "I bet she won't even remember me."

Jana's eyebrows pinched together when she looked at him. "Are you crazy? Of course she will."

"Why would she?"

"Because you have a very…distinct look."

Nate laughed. "That's a nice way of saying I'm a giant with a perpetual pen tucked behind my ear."

"You've only been carrying a pen since you started writing full-time." Jana held up her hands. "But you said it; I didn't."

He was used to Jana's teasing, and what she said was entirely the truth. As the firstborn son of two parents both over six foot, Nate towered over his family. And somehow,

Jana missed that gene on the DNA conveyor belt. The top of her head tucked nicely under his armpit.

As if his height wasn't obvious enough, Nate was often told he bore an uncanny resemblance to a blond Robert Downey, Jr. Not that he minded the comparison, but he never knew how to respond. Did he say "thanks," indirectly agreeing that he looked like RDJ? Should he ignore it and be thought a conceited jerk? He didn't know. He'd rather not be put on the spot.

"Seriously, if she doesn't recognize you as the tallest kid to walk the halls of Hendricks Elementary in the '90s, then she'll for sure remember you as the orneriest."

Jana's voice trailed off as Nate remembered Bethany as a spitfire. He liked her for that very reason. Not one to be overlooked, Bethany gave him an earful when she found out there was not a plastic ring for her. He remembered the flushed feeling on his face that seemed to set his hair on fire when she jabbed her pointer finger into his chest and called him stupid in front of the other girls. The embarrassment, even so many years later, was palpable.

Jana brushed her hands together. "I'm going to start on the bedroom closet. You finish up with the hutch and then we'll break for the day."

"Sounds good to me. Dinner out tonight?"

"Yes, but I think we need to shop again later. Eating out is killing my budget."

Nate set the drawer on the dining table and pulled out the chair, sitting down. "We can do that tonight after dinner." He looked up at her. "But first I'm going to finish up here and then check out that yoga studio."

Jana's eyes widened in mock warning. "You'd better find a ring somewhere first. Just to cover your bases."

MANIPURA YOGA WAS SQUEEZED IN BETWEEN A bike shop called Day Tripping to the west and Sturgeon Widows Tours to the east on Main Street in downtown Hendricks. It sported a yellow door, green-and-white-striped awning, and its name in flowing script across the wide picture window in front. Against the darkening sky, Bethany's studio was a sunflower, cheery and conspicuous. Nate tried to keep from smiling as he pushed open the front door.

Bethany had her back to him while she stood against the far wall. Even from a distance, Nate's gaze swept over her trim figure, a black T-shirt and lime leggings hugging her curves. One of her bare feet tapped out a rhythm to a tune only she could hear.

She still hadn't turned around even though the door chimes gave a clear indication that he'd entered the studio. For all she knew, he could be someone looking for directions or a serial killer or Robert Downey, Jr. himself. Nate ran a hand over his beard and unzipped his coat halfway. Either the studio was overly warm or his body temperature was hitting triple digits for other reasons.

Distracted, Bethany waved her hand in the air, addressing him. "I should have turned the sign around. We're closed. Normally that wouldn't be a big deal, someone walking in, but I've got this thing to get to and—"

Nate walked up to the counter, leaning forward to rest his elbows on the counter. "Remember me?"

Her foot stopped tapping. She turned around and stared at him for a full thirty seconds. Then she came closer until her hips pressed into the other side of the counter as she leaned forward to study his face. Was it his imagination or was she giving him a once-over for reasons other than trying to place his face? Actually, her scrutiny was more of a thrice-over.

"You look familiar," she said, squinting. Then after another ten seconds, "No. Sorry. Enlighten me."

Nate chuckled. "Here's a hint: you hated me in grade sch—"

"Nate Ransom? No way!"

"Weird, huh?"

She planted her hands on the counter and cocked her head. "You were head and shoulders taller than everyone in the school back then. Now—wait—what am I thinking? Come here."

Bethany came around the counter with her arms outstretched. Even as he sidestepped away from the counter, he pondered on how adulthood made it acceptable to hug your grade school adversary after not seeing him for seventeen years. He didn't dwell on it too long; Bethany wrapped her arms around him and the fleeting scent of eucalyptus and lemon chased the thought away.

When they separated, Bethany looked up at him, her smile wide and genuine. "I can't believe it's you. You look so...different. But the same." She waved the comment away. "That doesn't make any sense." She took another step back and her sweeping look at him, head to toe, almost set him on fire. "You're probably a full *body* taller than everyone."

Nate could barely take his eyes off her face. She was as pretty as ever. Her once long blonde hair was shorter, which only emphasized the angles of her face. And her eyes. They were the color of faded denim, slanting upward at the outer edges, almost disappearing above her full cheeks when she threw back her head and laughed. He'd been captivated by their color as a kid, and his fascination was no different now. The last he remembered, before his family moved to Duluth in seventh grade, she'd started filling out in all the right places. Of course she never noticed that he admired her from afar; she barely noticed him at all except for science lab assignments when they were paired up together. Bethany was cagey that way; she found the smartest people in each class they shared. Quiet and smart, Nate was one of those she sought out. He hadn't minded helping her even if she didn't talk to him outside of class. It had been a few years later, when he realized he'd been used all along.

"It makes perfect sense."

"What are you doing here? In Hendricks, I mean."

"My grandmother passed away in November."

Her eyebrows drew together. "That's right. Marcine Ransom. I'm so sorry."

Nate looked down at his shoes. "Thank you. She'd been sick. It wasn't a shock."

"Still. It was your grandma."

Nate shrugged. "Yes, and she was a great one too. But we're okay. I'm here with my sister packing up the house."

"So what have you been doing with yourself since

moving away from the hustle and bustle of Hendricks?" Bethany played with the keys in her hand. Their steely rustle punctuated the silent pauses between them.

"Finished school in Duluth. College in Arizona. Moved around for a few years after graduation. Now Duluth is my base while I travel."

"Marriage? Kids?" Bethany's smile seemed frozen.

"Neither, thankfully. Too busy."

Bethany's shoulders relaxed as she leaned back against the counter. "I know what you mean. Sometimes I think I teach classes in my sleep."

Nate looked around at the space. A bank of mirrors offset the yellow wall on the opposite side. The smooth, pale hardwood floor shone like a dull sun. It was a happy place—bright, spacious, serene.

"Congratulations. How long have you had your own studio?"

Her grin widened. "Thanks. Not very long. Since the summer." She snapped her fingers. "I'll have a men's class starting next week. Are you into yoga?"

"Me?" His voice cracked. She'd caught him off guard. "No. Never."

"Maybe you should start." The teasing lilt in her voice dared him to take her seriously. So she didn't expect him to take her up on it. Interesting.

"I'd turn your class into a comedy club."

She nodded slowly, studying his face. "Junior high seems like a lifetime ago, doesn't it?"

"No kidding. And one I wouldn't mind forgetting."

"I think I might have been kind of mean to you. Was I?"

Nate wasn't about to answer that. Not that he didn't want to revisit the past. In fact, he bet Bethany would be fun to reminisce with, but he wanted to hold off. It'd give them something to talk about next time.

Instead, he hooked his thumb over his shoulder. "Nah. I was joking about the hating thing. Listen, I won't keep you. Maybe we can catch up soon? Over dinner?"

Bethany scratched behind her ear. "Ah, sure. That'd be great."

"I'll be in touch."

"Looking forward to it."

Nate pushed open the door against the biting January wind. He glanced through the window into the well-lit studio as he walked past. Bethany sashayed across the room to switch off the light, and even after all this time, watching her move made his heart skip a beat. Showing up at her studio had gone better than he had planned. Had he really expected her to slug him or call him stupid again after all these years? The twelve-year-old in him admitted that, yes, it did cross his mind. Nate shoved his hand in his pocket to fish out his car keys.

Yes, it'd gone pretty well. He wondered how long he could wait until calling her for that dinner date.

Chapter Three

Bethany pushed the shovel along the sidewalk, exposing the red bricks under the fresh layer of snow. Fat flakes drifted lazily through the maple branches, dotting the sleeves of her red parka. According to her last look at the radar on her phone, more snow would be moving in around lunchtime.

The snow pile in front of her shovel grew until it tumbled over the top, so she stopped, scooped it up, and tossed it to the side of the path. Movement in the window at the back of her grandmother's house caught her attention, and when she glanced up, Donna Marconi's round, white face peered through the frosted glass of her bedroom window. Bethany waved.

The short path wound its way from the glorified garden shed that Bethany called home to Gran's two-bedroom bungalow forty feet away. It was Bethany's idea to move into the shed three years ago when she returned to Hendricks from Marquette. She and Gran both liked their independence but agreed Gran could use a little help in keeping the place from falling into disrepair after her broken hip fiasco. Surgery and months of therapy later, Gran still hadn't been able to mow her lawn and mop the floors. That was two years ago. And now, even with Gran fully recovered, she and Bethany fell into a state of easy coexistence. Moving to her own place became less and less important to Bethany.

Bethany didn't think of it as a shed but rather a studio apartment. Gran hired someone to fit it with plumbing and electricity and struck a deal with her neighbor friend to do the carpentry in exchange for Grandpa Joe's Chevy pickup. The shed had enough room for a kitchenette, a bathroom, and a small living space for her overstuffed futon that she'd splurged on. A wing chair reupholstered with a heavenly fuchsia brocade, a wood stove, and coffee table—a curbside find—filled the rest of the available space. Bethany draped the walls with woven tapestries that Gran had brought back from her South American travels and her own wall hangings that she'd woven at Handmakery, the folk art school in Dentsen, when she was going through her fiber artist period. A corner shelf held a few of Gran's pottery pieces when she moved onto wheel-throwing and ceramics. Bethany draped lights everywhere, too, and set candles on every available surface. Leave it to Gran to say Bethany's cozy home resembled the aftermath of an artist's studio hit by a tornado. Bethany loved it.

She did one last sweep of the walkway heading back

toward her studio then propped the shovel against the building's clapboard siding. Bethany grabbed her lukewarm coffee from the counter inside, stroked Silda's back when the cat wound itself around her legs, then closed the door behind her and headed toward Gran's back door. As soon as she entered the mudroom, the scent of cinnamon made her mouth water. Bethany knew something home-baked would soon be on the kitchen counter cooling if it wasn't already.

Up two short steps, Bethany pushed open the inside door leading into the kitchen. Gran worked with her back to Bethany. Her long black sweater swayed at her hips with the effort of whatever she was doing at the counter.

"Good morning, Gran."

Gran brushed floured hands on her black sweater and instantly swore when she'd realized what she'd done. Clouds of flour erupted from the fabric as she swiped at her sweater a few times. A splotch of flour decorated one cheek, and a chin-length strand of silver hair had escaped the black nylon rubber band at the base of her neck. Gran took baking seriously. Her appearance usually suffered for it.

"Any day I wake up with a heartbeat and two feet on the floor is a good one." Gran took the coffee pot from the hot plate and held it up in Bethany's direction. "Need a warm-up?"

Bethany held her mug under the pot until the dark, aromatic stream filled it near the brim. "Thank you."

Gran replaced the pot. "I saw your light still on when I got up around midnight. What kept you up?"

Bethany lifted her shoulders. "Just watching a movie."

The older woman squinted at her with one eye open, the other closed. "That Justin guy wasn't over?"

"*That's* been over for weeks. Where have you been?"

"How am I supposed to know? You don't tell me anything." Gran suppressed a smile behind her own coffee cup.

"Gran! So untrue! I tell you everything." Bethany looked down at her feet. "Sort of."

"See?"

"You should be thankful. You wouldn't like me telling you *everything*."

Gran raised her eyebrows and turned back to the counter, plucking muffins out of the tin and setting them on a plate to cool. Bethany smiled at the easy banter, typical of their conversations about Bethany's love life. Or lack of was more like it.

Bethany inherited her grandmother's willowy figure and her sass; she was grateful for both traits. But they also shared an aversion to long-term relationships with the opposite sex. In fairness to Gran, Bethany knew her grandmother was a devoted wife to her late husband, Joe, who made her a widow more than twenty years ago. After he died, Gran dated occasionally but never found anyone to replace her one true love. Bethany supposed Gran had been lonely and wasn't really looking for someone to replace him. The length of time between dates grew wider and wider until Gran stopped seeing men altogether. Bethany couldn't remember the last time Gran went out with someone. Her independence fit her like a glove. She'd grown accustomed to being alone.

Unlike Gran, Bethany had yet to find her soulmate, and it was no wonder—the idea of a committed relationship gave her a bad taste in her mouth. Gran often chided her granddaughter to not dismiss the guys she dated before she got to know them, and admittedly Bethany ditched quite a few. Especially the nice guys. In fact, the more ideal the guy, the louder her warning bells sounded. She liked to tell herself that she feared losing her independence, but that wasn't the most honest reason. She knew that. No, her fear of rejection kept the nice guys at arm's length, and protected her in the process. If she broke it off first, Bethany would save herself the heartache.

Bethany plucked a warm muffin off the plate in the middle of the table and set it on her napkin. "Just so you can't accuse me of keeping secrets, here's something interesting: I was at the studio last night closing up and guess who walked in?"

Gran wiped her hands on a towel and sat down opposite Bethany. "Who?"

"Nate Ransom. He moved away in junior high." Bethany looked down at her fingers wrapped around her mug so she wouldn't see Gran's eyes light up at the new prospect.

"Yes," she purred. "Marcine's grandson. He was a cutie when he was younger. Has he changed much?"

"Gran. He's a grown man now. Of course, he's changed."

"Don't be coy with me. You know exactly what I mean."

Bethany looked away, feigning disinterest. When she glanced back at Gran, the older woman scrutinized her through squinty eyes.

She sighed. "Fine. Yes, he's really, really good-looking. There. Happy?"

"But when will you two go out?"

"Cut to the chase, why don't you?"

"I'm done beating around the bush with you," Gran said with a wink. "With my luck, I'll have one foot in the grave by the time I get you married off."

"Well, we're *not* getting married. We're just going to dinner sometime soon to catch up."

Gran looked toward the window, a shadow crossing over her face. "That's too bad about Marcine. She was a sweetheart. I imagine he's here taking care of the house? I don't envy that job. Marcine was quite the collector."

"Yes, he'll be in town awhile, I think."

"What kind of work does he do?" Gran wiped her hand across her brow then rested her elbow on the table.

"We didn't get that far." She studied Gran. "Are you okay?"

Gran waved her hand in the air, not looking at Bethany. "Meaning you didn't ask him. Too busy talking about yourself?"

Bethany tilted her head, looking at her grandmother incredulously. "I'm not the narcissist you think I am. He came in just as I was about to lock up."

"What do you know about him then, aside from the fact that he's clearing Marcine's house?"

"He lives in Duluth. He went to college in Arizona." Bethany ticked each one off on her fingers. "Not married. No kids. That's it."

Gran clasped her hands together at her chest. "Thank

goodness you at least had the sense to get the important stuff."

"Right? I'm not completely hopeless. He just kept firing questions at me."

"Do you need another refresher on how not to be the center of attention?"

Bethany fluffed her hair. "I can't help myself." Then Bethany dropped her hands in her lap. "Please, Gran. You know me better than that."

Gran tapped the tabletop with her fingertips. "I'm just teasing you." She collected Bethany's empty mug and carried it to the sink. "I'm sure you two will have a grand time if you give him the time of day."

It occurred to Bethany as she watched Gran cross the kitchen that she moved slower than usual. "Are you sure you're feeling okay? You seem tired."

Gran set the mug in the sink and turned on the water. "I'm fine. I think my body wants to hibernate or something."

Bethany watched her grandmother for a few seconds in silence. "Well, I think you're just reading into Nate and me a little more than you need to."

"He wouldn't bother with just anyone." Gran wagged a finger at her. "He must have liked you."

Bethany blew out an exaggerated breath. "According to you, they all like me."

"I don't doubt that."

"Maybe he's just looking for someone to spend downtime with while he's here. Packing up an entire house would be tedious work. I'm a diversion."

"There you go, trying to talk yourself out of liking him before you've even had your first date."

"There *you* go, trying to marry me off to the next guy between twenty and fifty who blows into town."

Gran chuckled and kissed the top of Bethany's head when she passed by her. "You know me too well."

Bethany pulled apart the muffin, watching the steam rise from its middle. Maybe she'd given a thought or two to she and Nate having dinner, whenever that would be. It was a curious feeling, meeting someone so many years after you'd last seen him, searching for the boy underneath the guise of adulthood. She remembered how upset her eight-year-old self had been when she'd found out that Nate Ransom gave stupid plastic rings, the kind that cost a quarter in the bubblegum machine, to all of her friends in third grade except her. It was such a trivial thing, looking back on it, but it was a tremendous hurt to an eight-year-old. Hot, angry tears burned her cheeks that day as she hid against the wall of the school behind the bucket of recess balls. No one asked where she was when the class was called back inside after recess. Her friends had been too busy gushing about their gaudy plastic treasures, compliments of the freckled-face jerk with the missing front tooth, Nate Ransom. She hated him from that day forward.

She smiled now at the memory. Nothing would come of this "date," so Gran shouldn't get worked up about it. No, they'd simply be catching up for an hour or two. They'd hug and tell each other how nice it was to see each other, say their goodbyes. Then he'd ready his grandmother's house for auction and get back to his life in Duluth afterward. One month was the ideal length for a relationship in her mind, and the obstacle of an impossible long-distance relationship was the perfect built-in excuse to keep them apart.

Gran's wishful thinking radar was overreacting again as usual.

Chapter Four

Nate waited three days to call Bethany to ask if she'd like to grab dinner somewhere, and it took every fiber of patience to wait that long. When he'd finally quashed his fear that she'd turn him down, he called the studio before he lost the nerve. Bethany didn't hesitate, saying she'd like to go with him.

Twenty minutes before he was due at Bethany's place, Nate swooped into the kitchen, a navy tie trailing over his shoulder and his shirt hem untucked.

"What do you think?"

He was still stuffing the material into his waistband when Jana turned away from the sink. She gave him a cool appraisal. "Not bad. You are going to wear the tie around your neck, right?"

He glanced at his shoulder where the tie hung and snagged it off. "Almost forgot. Thanks."

Jana took a plate out of the dishwasher and replaced it in the cabinet. "Where are you taking her?"

"Fernando's."

"That's an awfully expensive place for a little catch-up conversation." She focused on putting dishes away, but a little smile played across her lips.

"No one can accuse me of being cheap." He hoped to make an impression and Fernando's was the logical choice.

Jana gave him a sideways look. "Uh-huh. If I weren't just your clueless little sister, I'd say you're hoping for a little more than an hour or two of reminiscing."

"Meaning—?"

"I mean being in Hendricks for as long as it takes to pack up the house might not be long enough for you and Bethany Marconi."

He looked down at Jana whose smug expression made him chuckle. "I'm not planning on anything at this point, being that I haven't seen her since seventh grade. She might actually be a pretty obnoxious person."

"And what you're saying is you won't be able to stand an hour in her company let alone two?"

He shrugged. "Exactly."

Jana blew air out of her mouth. "Who are you trying to kid? You've done nothing but stumble around in a daze these past few days since going to her studio."

Nate cringed. "I've been doing that? Pathetic."

"Tell me about it."

Nate finished knotting his tie then checked his phone. "Gotta run. Don't wait up."

Jana closed the door of the dishwasher. "Now don't

overwhelm her with your questions. You're not on the job tonight."

"I'll let her get one question in for every three of mine."

"A two-to-one ratio might ensure a second date."

Nate gave his sister a one-armed hug. "Good point."

BETHANY HAD FORGOTTEN ABOUT NATE RANSOM until the phone rang during an intermediate yoga class yesterday morning. She didn't answer it; she never did during active sessions. But when she checked her voicemail after class, pen in hand to take notes if needed, and heard his voice, a low timbre that reminded her of the freight trains rumbling on the tracks near her apartment in Marquette years ago, she set the pen down. He wondered if she was free the next night. Would she like to go to Fernando's in Two Rivers? Could she call him back when she got a free minute? Of course. Of course. Of course.

When she returned the call, they'd settled on a time that he'd pick her up—six o'clock. Now it was the next night, ten minutes to six, and Bethany paced the minuscule space between her kitchen counter and the east window where, if she stood on her futon and looked out the uppermost part of the window, she could see over the fence to the street. Nate drove a red Range Rover he said when she told him she'd watch for him so he wouldn't have to come through the gate to her studio. Bethany didn't want to trouble him, but she was also just a little bit self-conscious at first, like she was with anybody new she dated. Her home was no bigger than a large bedroom, and at twenty-nine, sometimes she felt she should have more to show for herself.

Headlights swept across the gaps in the fence as Nate pulled to the curb. Bethany grabbed her bag and was out the door and through the gate before he got any ideas about coming in for her.

Nate stood by the passenger-side door, gripping the door handle. "I hope you don't mind that our reservations aren't until seven. I should have called the restaurant sooner."

Bethany hopped into the passenger seat. "That's fine. We'll have plenty of time to catch up."

After he closed her door, she peered through the windshield and followed him as he circled around to his door. She caught a fleeting glimpse of the boy she remembered so many years ago, the small, straight nose, the sand-colored, bottle-brush hair, and those eyes—dark and black-lashed, too, with straight, full brows which lent him a serious expression—and then the image floated away with the blast of cold air that hit her when he opened his door. Bethany pulled her collar tight against the chill, but warmth spread through her from the bottom up. She smiled. He'd turned the seat warmer on for her.

Twenty minutes later they found two empty seats at the bar in Fernando's, a place to reconnect until their table was ready. The restaurant was a maze of small rooms, wood-paneled and warmed by candlelight. The drifting notes of piano music somewhere in the restaurant lent its lazy notes to the tranquil mood, despite a steady hum of voices. Bethany had only been to Fernando's a handful of times, and she wondered why she didn't eat there more often. The place had a cool vibe and was known for its seafood.

Bethany tugged the neck of her sweater toward her collarbone. She'd worn it because claret complemented her skin tone, but now she regretted its low scoop neck after the bartender looked pointedly at her before and after he took their order. It wasn't her usual style, but the new sweater seemed to fit better in the store. Slumping was out of the question tonight.

Nate cleared his throat and shifted on his stool, looking at her profile. "So, you live with your grandmother?"

Though his question held no hint of sarcasm, a flush crept up Bethany's neck. Again, those insecurities got the better of her sometimes when she least expected them.

"Yes. Actually, it's a little studio apartment in the backyard. I help her out a lot. She's had health issues."

"I bet she loves having you there."

"She does, and I love being there."

"Grandparents are great. My sister and I were really close to my dad's parents," he said, looking into his glass. "I miss them both." Nate turned to study her. "I'm surprised I haven't run into you before now with as many times as I've come back to Hendricks since we moved away."

"After high school, I was gone for about seven years. I went to school in Marquette, and then when I graduated, I stayed there for a few more years to work. I've only been back in Hendricks three years."

"Still, I'm surprised." Nate eyes lingered on her until the bartender brought Bethany's drink.

Again, the bartender's eyes dipped to Bethany's neckline

before she had a chance to clutch the silver fern pendant as a shield. She glared at him before he turned away.

Bethany glanced back at Nate. "Well, it's not like you were looking for me when you came to Hendricks, right?"

Nate's expression changed and he looked away for a few seconds. When he turned toward her again, he smiled. "No, I guess I wasn't."

An awkward silence hung between them. Bethany wished she could take back the comment while she swirled her ice around inside the glass with a spoon. She needed to come up with something fast. Silence was never a good thing on a first date.

"So, what do you do for work?"

Nate straightened on his stool. "I write. Mostly for the *Duluth Herald*, but I've transitioned to part time while I take on more freelance stuff. Travel magazines and websites are my bread and butter now. It's taken awhile to build up a list of regular gigs, but I'm doing all right."

"Nice. So…you travel a lot?"

"Not as much as the job title implies. I take two big trips every year, and then use them to generate content for a bunch of different outlets. I'll travel more once I go full time."

"What's your favorite place that you've been to?"

Nate closed an eye and looked to the ceiling, thinking. "For the scenery: Norway. Sicily has the best food. Tokyo, the friendliest people. My all-time favorite big city is Chicago."

"Mine, too, though I'm not really a city person. Marquette was big enough for me."

"I know what you mean," he said, encircling his glass with his hands. "Big cities are nice to visit. I get a little claustrophobic if I'm visiting for more than a few days. Have you traveled much?"

"I've been to maybe ten states. Oh, and one too-long trip to London with my parents when I was ten, but only because my grandmother was in the hospital and they had no one else to leave me with."

"Your parents went overseas when your grandmother was in the hospital?"

Bethany waved her hand dismissively. "It wasn't a vacation. They went there for business."

"Still. She was in the hospital."

Bethany looked down at her lap. "My parents, they—" She gritted her teeth. "They don't always handle things the way you or I would."

Nate bumped her lightly in the shoulder with his own. "Sorry to press."

Their table ready, the hostess led them through the restaurant to a small room with four other tables. Nate offered her the seat closest to the stone fireplace and she sighed, instantly grateful. The place was chilly and her sweater thin. Inside the hearth a fire crackled, and the heady scent of burnt oak filled Bethany's senses.

When Nate sat down, his knees knocked on the underside of the table, sending the salt-and-pepper dispensers tumbling on their sides. At Nate's height, Bethany bet he ran into a few logistical problems with his long legs. He set them upright and looked sheepishly at her. The waitress came by, handed them menus, and went over the specials. Bethany studied Nate as he asked about an entree on the menu. He reminded her of someone, a movie star, but she couldn't think of his name. It would come to her she knew, at some strange time, like elusive thoughts usually did.

After the waitress hurried away, Bethany noticed the grin playing on Nate's lips as he watched her.

"What are you smiling about?" She couldn't help but smile herself.

"Just thinking back to when we were in school."

"It seems like another lifetime, doesn't it?"

"Some things I remember like they happened yesterday."

Do you remember Mr. Frietag? Sixth-grade science?"

"He loved me."

"All the teachers loved you because you were a brain."

Nate threw back his head and laughed. He had such nice straight teeth. *Who did he remind her of?*

Bethany smoothed the napkin across her lap. "Anyway, he lived next to us until they sold their house and moved to Florida. He scared me to death in the classroom. Such a great neighbor though."

Nate's brow creased. "Why were you scared of him?"

"Because he never smiled. Dead serious all the time. And he called on me even though I never raised my hand."

"Maybe that's why he called on you. To see if you were paying attention."

"I was."

His eyes bore into hers. "I would argue that you were paying more attention to who was paying attention to you."

"What's that supposed to mean?" Her voice rose

unintentionally, and she looked around the room to see if anyone noticed.

"It means you liked being the center of attention. And you were good at it."

"How so?" *Was he calling her a show-off?*

"Some people crave attention and they're just obnoxious about it. Everyone was drawn to you," Nate said, tapping the top of his glass with his index finger. He arched an eyebrow. "Me included."

Bethany leaned back in her seat and crossed her arms. "Now you're just playing with me. If that were true, I would have had a ring to show for it."

Again, Nate's laughter rang throughout the small space. This time, people did look. His dark eyes caught the candlelight and—

She snapped her fingers. "Robert Downey, Jr."

Nate's brows bunched together. "Excuse me?"

"That's who you remind me of. I've been trying to come up with his name for fifteen minutes."

"I hear that a lot."

"He's one of my favorite actors," she said, and instantly regretted it. It sounded so moony, so unlike her. Now he'd think she agreed to the date because he looked like Robert Downey, Jr. Where had her composure gone tonight?

Their waitress returned and took their orders. Bethany pressed on her stomach to ease the rumble of hunger pains. She'd skipped lunch in the rush to run errands around town. While she could probably polish off two entrees without effort, she settled for the bourbon honey salmon.

Their waitress collected their menus and left, and Bethany's gaze returned to Nate.

He looked pointedly at her, an elbow resting on the table, chin in hand. "You're still bitter, aren't you?"

"How could I not be? I was the only girl in third grade who didn't get one!"

"Maybe it's twenty years too late, but I'm really sorry. It wasn't intentional." He folded his hands together on the table. "I was so nervous you'd laugh at me that I handed them out to everyone, saving you for last. And I lost it somewhere."

"You could have bought another."

"You chewed me out before I had the chance."

"I hated you for that until you moved away."

"Yes, you made that very clear."

Bethany smiled, twisting the opal ring on her finger, a birthday gift from Gran. "If you told me you'd lost it, I still wouldn't have believed you."

"Grudges die hard, don't they?"

"Indeed."

The corners of Nate's mouth dipped despite the lighthearted conversation, and Bethany realized maybe he took her teasing to heart. Was he really wrestling with something that happened in *grade school*? Again, she wracked her brain to change the topic lest the night turn into one tense moment after another. She was about to ask him about his sister when he spoke up.

"So, do your parents still live here?"

"No, they haven't for a while. I think they bought their

condo in Minneapolis while I was in first grade." She smiled at his blank expression.

"But you stayed in Hendricks?"

"Yes. Hence, my closeness to Gran. My parents lived in the city during the week and in Hendricks on the weekends."

Nate looked down at his folded hands. She could tell he struggled with what to say next by the way his forehead wrinkled. He opened his mouth to speak, but then the waitress came back with a basket of bread, and they spent the next few minutes silently buttering warm rolls.

"That must have been hard, living separately from your parents for most of your life," he said quietly.

Bethany set the rest of her roll down and wiped her fingers on the napkin in her lap, wanting to avoid Nate's eyes. The subject of her parents was a tricky topic. She didn't talk about them much.

"It was like that for as long as I could remember. That was my normal. I'm especially thankful for Gran in hindsight." Bethany cleared her throat, ready to move on to something else.

"Hopefully they made up on weekends for the time they were gone?"

She smiled. "Sometimes."

He frowned. "Do you want to talk about something else?"

Bethany warmed at the sympathetic expression that crossed his face. "If you don't mind. Maybe a more lighthearted topic is better for a first date."

The waitress returned with their food, so a few minutes

passed while their plates were set before them, and a waiter came by to fill their water glasses. Still, Nate kept glancing at her like he was anxious to resume the conversation. And sure enough, as soon as the servers left, Nate's eyebrows shot up.

"First date?"

"Isn't that what this is?"

"First implies there will be a second."

Bethany stared at him and Nate stared right back. She was no stranger to flirting, but he made her feel self-conscious for some reason. Something around the eyes, pronounced laugh lines and the coal dark irises gave him a playful air that Bethany found a little irresistible. Actually, *a lot* irresistible.

By the time they finished eating, two hours had passed. Nate was easy to talk to. If he wasn't living in Duluth, Bethany might consider keeping him around longer than she usually allowed herself. The distance between Duluth and Hendricks was the saving grace, though. Maybe they'd see each other again; maybe they wouldn't.

Either way, Bethany decided to keep Nate Ransom at arm's length until he went back to Duluth for good. If she looked hard enough, faults aplenty would surface. They always did, no matter who she dated. And Nate seemed *too* nice, *too* perfect—a throwback to the boy she crushed on before the ring debacle. She might need an extra month or two to come up with a plausible reason why she couldn't keep him around.

No, Nate was definitely not anyone she'd spend time mooning over. The sooner he left town, the better.

Chapter Five

Snow blanketed the cars parked overnight along Main Street. Bethany squinted at the harsh light and looked down at her feet until she remembered her sunglasses in the bag swinging at her hip. She fumbled for them and sighed with relief when she put them on. As Bethany walked to her studio, she realized the snow-draped cars reminded her of a trip to Europe she took with Gran when she was twelve. What made the biggest impression on her during those three weeks were the thermal baths they found in Egerszalok, Turkey. The steaming pools had been surrounded by limestone hills, colossal formations like white, silent giants standing against an impossibly blue sky much like the cars appeared this morning. The memory made her sad for some reason, and she pushed it from her mind, concentrating on her boots crunching on the salted sidewalk.

Ahead, Ethan Day unlocked the door to Day Tripping,

the bike shop next to Bethany's studio, but he stepped back when he watched her approach.

"Good morning!" His voice cracked the silence.

She sighed loudly. "Is it? I wasn't sure."

Bethany drew closer and smiled in spite of her mood. Ethan had that effect on her. As her neighbor next door to the studio, she and Ethan referred to each other as "my Main Street buddy."

"Ouch," he said, taking her in from head to toe. "Someone is standing on the wrong side of the bed. There's still time for a do-over."

Ethan didn't deserve such a clipped response; she was instantly sorry and said so.

"It's just that today seems like a continuation of last night and the night before."

Ethan frowned. "Uh-oh. Who was the lucky guy this time?"

"I think I've mentioned him last week. Nate Ransom?"

"Yes, you did. I can't keep track."

He held the door for her to the bike shop and she stepped inside all the while glaring at him.

"Ethan, darling, that's not a helpful comment."

"Sorry," he offered without an ounce of sympathy in his tone. "Not a good date then?"

Bethany's shoulders dropped and she looked at the ceiling. "On the contrary, it was pretty darned awesome."

"Wait. There's a disconnect somewhere."

"'Disconnect' could sum up my life."

Ethan nodded slowly and kept a watchful eye on her. "I

see. You like him *too* much. And that doesn't fit into the Bethany Marconi playbook."

She pointed at him. "Bingo."

"After all these years I'm still not sure about your self-sabotaging drama."

Bethany followed him around the store while he moved through the process of opening the shop—turning on the neon window sign, the music, and checking the charge of the tablet at the counter. He managed the bike shop for Charles and Dora Eggleston, who lived permanently in Boca Raton now, but kept the shop open since it was a Hendricks mainstay. Thankfully, the shop stayed in the black between equipment sales and bike rentals April through October, but it was also in part to Ethan's marketing prowess. If he wasn't posting on one of the shop's social media platforms, he was sponsoring an event along the North Shore. People traveled from all over to buy or get bikes serviced at Day Tripping. Ethan's wiry frame bespoke of the hours he spent on a bike, too, so he understood the biking culture like he knew the palm of his hand. The shop buzzed with constant business.

"It's not drama. It's just that liking this guy isn't practical."

"This is big for you, admitting that you like someone," he said, disappearing into the office to flip on the lights before he came back out to check messages on the answering machine.

"Oh, I like a lot of them. I just don't want to keep them around."

Ethan paused, his finger hovering over the button to play messages. "And why isn't it practical?"

Bethany rested her elbows on the counter. "He moves back to Duluth in a month. And long-distance love is an even bigger no-no."

Ethan studied her. "Here's a novel idea: how about *not* writing him off just yet even though keeping him around goes against all of your self-imposed *rules*?" He hooked his fingers in the air at the word "rules."

She squinted at him. "You think my rules are frivolous, don't you?"

He paused for a few seconds. "I think you should just give him a chance."

"I don't want to lead him—"

"Worry about that at the end of the month."

Bethany watched a plow rumble past the store, snow fanning out ahead of it. "You know, you're right. I feel like living dangerously for once."

Ethan wrinkled his nose. "Some might argue that's not dangerous. It's safe. You know, being with people you like?" He checked his phone. "Don't you have a class starting soon?"

"Are you trying to shoo me out of the shop?" Bethany pressed her palms together when he looked defensive. "I'm kidding. No, it doesn't start until eleven. But Darcy left a message that she'd be stopping by, so I'd better scoot."

He came around from behind the counter and gave her a hug. Bethany's chin rested easily on Ethan's shoulder as she embraced her friend. "I hope your day gets better," he said.

Bethany kissed him on the cheek. "It will. Thanks for listening as usual."

She turned to leave, and with one hand on the door, she paused. Ethan's eyebrows rose when she looked back at him.

"How come you've never asked me out on a date?"

He squinted at her. "I asked three years ago. You shot me down. Why does it not surprise me that you don't remember that?"

Bethany winced. "Sorry. Thanks for still being my friend."

Ethan waved her off. "Get out of my shop before I start to second-guess myself."

DARCY SHOWED UP A HALF HOUR LATER, LOOKING fresh-faced yet wearing a mismatched outfit in need of an iron. Underneath the parka, her faded denim overalls and oversized flannel shirt were clearly from another era, faded and threadbare in spots. She'd tucked the pant legs into her mid-calf boots, but the extra material and the boots' Sherpa lining gave Darcy's calves a sausage effect. Bethany hadn't talked to her since Darcy called in a panic about the fight she'd had with Sean. Maybe her friend was swimming in the depths of depression, and this outfit was the sad result.

Bethany scratched her head. "I hate to say it, but this look isn't your best."

Darcy spread her arms wide. "What, you don't like the mid-century, hand-me-down trend. It's so in right now."

"I've never been particularly fashionable. You're one up on me."

Darcy laughed, hooking her thumbs in the bibs's hip pockets. "I'm helping Sean around the inn today. We're sanding the floors upstairs. I just ran into town to pick something up for lunch later."

"So, you two obviously fixed what was broken since I haven't had any more calls for help," Bethany said, switching on the scent warmer in the corner of the studio. Whenever the scent of eucalyptus filled the room and the instrumental track she used before the start of class played, an instant sense of peace settled on her shoulders. Bethany needed that more than anything at the moment. If only she could shake this mood.

"Yes. You were right. We both apologized. It's all good."

"See? Told you."

"You also told me that you weren't good at giving relationship advice."

"It was a fluke."

"Fluke or not, thanks."

"For what it took to get you two together, it's time well spent."

"Speaking of time, I came to remind you about the Red Hot Gala. I have two tickets with your name on them," she said, pulling the tickets from her pocket and waving them at Bethany. "Find anyone to bring yet?"

Bethany spun away from Darcy so her friend wouldn't see her grit her teeth. She didn't want to think about asking her only prospect at the moment to a formal event on the most romantic weekend of the year. She slipped the tickets into her jacket pocket.

"So that's a no?" Darcy came up behind Bethany and inched around her to stand right in her face. "Or is that a yes?"

Avoiding Darcy when she wore that needling look on her face was impossible. She was stubborn that way. And Darcy knew Bethany well enough to know that she would have a date for something like this. Bethany didn't like to miss the Red Hot Gala because it meant dressing up for a change. It meant a small yet elegant respite and a consolation for living in Hendricks during the brutally cold, unforgiving winters.

"Okay." Darcy crossed her arms. "Who is it?"

Bethany sighed. "Actually, it's someone pretty amazing. I went to school with him. Can you believe that? He came back to town to settle his grandmother's estate. And he just walked into the studio last week. We've been out once, and—"

Bethany was gushing. It was so unlike her that she clamped her mouth shut. Too late. Darcy's megawatt grin could power the North Shore.

"Wow, Beth. This guy might be the one. Can't wait to meet him."

Bethany lifted a shoulder. "It's not that serious. Like I said, we've been on one date."

Darcy's smile only widened. "You are so full of it. Look at you. Your face is red! I've never seen you blush."

Bethany rubbed her cheeks, disappointed that she could be so easily read. "That's because I don't and I'm not." When Darcy's smile faltered, guilt overcame Bethany.

"Okay, look. His name's Nate Ransom, and he's a great guy from what I can tell, but he lives in Duluth. I'm not even sure he'll be around for the Gala."

"You could ask him and find out. Even if he isn't still in Hendricks, Duluth isn't that far away."

"He won't want to drive four hours round trip for a five-hour benefit."

"Yes, he will if he looked you up after all these years." Darcy cocked her head to the side. "Promise me you'll ask."

"Fine."

The doorbell chimed. Emily Stetman, owner of Sturgeon Widows Tours and a shorter, silver-haired lady who Bethany didn't recognize walked in for the first class.

Darcy waved at Emily, Sean's mom, then turned back to Bethany.

"Listen. I won't keep you," she said, zipping her coat. "Tell me what he says when you ask him. Got it?"

Why did she confide in Darcy about this? "Yes, I'll call him as soon as class is over. Thanks for the tickets."

Satisfied, Darcy left the studio. Bethany watched her friend get into Sean's pickup truck and drive away. She took a deep breath to ease the tension that gripped her shoulders, knotted her stomach. For the same old reason, asking Nate to go to the Red Hot Gala made her nervous. She'd be setting herself up for disappointment, and she hated more than anything to be vulnerable, to give someone other than herself the power to be in control.

Chapter Six

Twenty-nine years old and still stuck on the girl he crushed on in grade school.

After their date at Fernando's the other night, Bethany cemented herself as a permanent fixture in his mind. His crush had come roaring back all these years even though she'd barely agreed to a second date. But he'd noticed the signs: the easy banter, the Robert Downey, Jr. reference, the lingering looks. Nate wasn't sure she was serious when she casually hinted at a second date. Maybe she wanted his reaction, but Nate was willing to risk the humiliation of being turned down when he asked for another date.

Nate sighed as he pulled into a parking spot in the public lot at D & G Grocery, a half-block away from Bethany's yoga studio. It was a quarter to eleven, almost time for her first session of the day. If she didn't laugh him out of the studio before class started, he'd break something before the hour was over. What was he doing? He'd surely make a fool of himself.

He sidestepped the icy patches on the sidewalk as he made his way to the studio. Two women walked ahead of him, each carrying a rolled mat and a water bottle swinging in unison at their sides. *Great. Two more audience members for the Nate Ransom Yoga Comedy Hour.*

As he walked the last few steps, he rehearsed in his head how he'd ask her. Another date with Bethany was definitely worth the risk of rejection. He wasn't the skinny, awkward kid anymore. He could handle the word "no." And if there was a chance for a second date, *he'd* have to ask her. Nate knew that as sure as he knew his own name. It wasn't out of some old-fashioned notion that women didn't call guys for dates either. No way, not her. Bethany didn't have to ask because guys called *her*. Her casual indifference was the allure. Cool and charismatic. Even when he'd known her in grade school, kids buzzed around her like worker bees did a queen. She hadn't changed.

So here he was. Game enough to twist his appendages in ways they weren't meant to bend, desperate for some more of her time. He wasn't sure if this was the way to Bethany's heart, but trying wouldn't hurt.

When he opened the door and walked in, Bethany's mouth literally dropped open like a marionette.

"Are you serious?!" Bethany said aloud—really loud—but then clasped her hand to her mouth. She didn't say another word until she was shoulder to shoulder with him. "I'm so sorry," she mumbled. "That was really unprofessional of me. Did that just sink my review on Yelp?"

Nate's brain scrambled for a moment. Her eyes were lit from within, radiant and full of life. "You can redeem yourself if you don't laugh at me in the next hour."

"Deal," she said, looking at the other class members who were already unrolling mats on the floor. "I didn't think yoga was your thing?"

"Did I say that?"

She looked him over. "No, I guess you didn't."

He couldn't help but laugh at her candor. "I'm trying to embrace new things. New Year's resolution and all that." He scouted a place in the back of the room so he wouldn't be so conspicuous. "I'd better grab that spot before I get stuck up front. Where should I put my stuff?" Nate unzipped his jacket and tried to keep a straight face when her eyes drifted to his chest. He knew how he looked in a tank. Bethany's widened eyes confirmed it.

"Your stuff?" Bethany asked distractedly. "Oh! Yes, sorry. There are cubbies in the back of the room. There are mats to borrow back there, too, if you need one."

"Good enough." He turned away, but said over his shoulder, "Go easy on me, okay?"

"No guarantees," she said, a one-sided grin playing on her lips.

Nate stuffed his coat and shoes in the cubicle and peeled off his sweats, revealing his compression pants underneath. The fabric hugged his body, and suddenly more eyes were on him than he bargained for. Maybe signing up for a men's-only class would have been a better idea.

Bethany glided across the room, willowy and erect, smiling in that half-amused way that pinched the skin together between her eyebrows and made people smile back. She pushed her bangs aside, and winked at him. Nate might spontaneously combust if she did that again.

"Welcome to Yoga 101, everyone," she said. "Let's get started before our morning coffee wears off, shall we?"

Murmurs of agreement echoed in the room.

Nate knelt on the floor mat and didn't quite know what to do with his arms or legs. The women on either side of him had already twisted themselves into painful-looking sitting positions. There was no earthly way Nate would ever be able to copy them without tearing a ligament.

Across the room, Bethany seemed to sense his reservations because she smiled at him when he caught her eye.

"If you're new to yoga, do what you can. We'll work on perfecting your form when I meet with you privately during the next few weeks. What we are trying to do is help you find what's comfortable for you at this point. So, relax and enjoy."

What a relief.

Nate was surprised at how quickly the time moved. When she wasn't speaking into her headset at the front of the room, Bethany hovered over him most of the time, correcting his form or explaining the origin of the poses.

An hour later, the two women who walked into the studio ahead of him were the last to leave. Nate purposefully stalled so he and Bethany could be alone. He stood at his cubby, his back to her, zipping and unzipping his sweatshirt. When that got old, Nate kneeled to tie and retie his shoes. He listened to her conversation with the other students as they left, and soon the sound of bare feet on the mats behind him told him she was near.

Bethany stopped next to him, crossing her arms. "So why did you really come here today?"

"Maybe to learn how to relax." He looked up at her as he tied the strings on his sweats, something he never did. He doubted she'd buy that explanation. In a list of a hundred traits, "anxious" wouldn't be on there to describe him. Seeing her now, even with her hair askew and a sheen of sweat showing across her collarbone, Bethany made him think twice about what he meant to say. Nate struggled to not trip over his tongue every time he opened his mouth.

"You don't seem so uptight to me." It wasn't an accusation. By the tone of her voice, Bethany was playing him.

He stood up. "Oh, I keep it under the surface."

"I see." Her eyes raked him from head to toe.

They stared at each other until Bethany blinked and broke the spell.

She drummed her fingers against her bicep. "You're a terrible liar."

Nate leaned back against the counter, resting his elbows on the surface behind him. "Go out with me again."

"What will we do?" she asked as if her answer depended on what he could offer.

He squinted at her, thinking. "So many options to choose from in Hendricks. Let's see." He paused, enjoying her amused expression. "Movie at the Regency. Coffee at Two Tree. We could picnic on the beach."

"It's winter."

"You've never had a winter picnic?"

"I'm a summer picnic kind of girl."

"How have you lived this long without enjoying the experience?"

"That's an experience that I'll do without, thanks."

"That just gave me the best idea."

"I repeat: I only eat meals outside when it's above sixty degrees. I don't like being cold."

"So that's a 'yes'?"

Bethany shrugged, giving in, though Nate knew she wasn't taking him seriously. "Sure. What should I wear?"

Nate rubbed his hands together. "Something warm."

Her bugged-eyed look as he put on his coat left no doubt that his idea would be a winner. She followed him to the door.

"Did you not understand me?" she said after him. "No outdoor activities. I'm not a fan!"

He opened the door. "I'm determined to make you the biggest fan. I'll call you."

"I won't be going!" Her voice trailed onto the sidewalk before the door shut behind him, and the lightness of her voice assured him that she wasn't dead set against the idea.

In fact, once Bethany realized the effort his plan took, she'd know how crazy he was about her. If he knew anything about Bethany in the short time they'd spent together, he understood she liked feeling special. And what he planned for their date would certainly make her feel like a queen. Maybe an ice queen, but like royalty nonetheless.

Chapter Seven

Two mornings later Bethany woke up with the sheets tangled around her hips and cold perspiration pasting the ends of her hair to her face and neck. She looked around her room, which was brightened by the morning's blush on the horizon. At first she didn't know what woke her. She listened for a sound. But then the details of the dream began to float back into her consciousness. Bethany lay back against the pillow, closing her eyes, letting the dream take shape in her mind's eye.

She'd had a version of the dream earlier in the week too. It was her birthday. Everyone came—her parents, Gran, Darcy and Sean, Ethan, even people she hadn't seen for years. Nate was there too. She sat at the head of a long table. A cake, one of those many-layered wedding cakes, sat in front of her with candles all over. Hundreds of candles. Everyone began to sing happy birthday to her, but the candles remained unlit. So Bethany stopped everyone from singing to light them, but the silk flower petals caught fire. In a rush, the flames consumed the cake, the table, and the room, sweeping from one end of the room to the other like a tidal wave. Her family and friends escaped the fire, but her legs were so heavy, as if glue adhered her feet to the floor. She stood at the front door, unable to take the last few steps to safety, feeling the heat at her back. Bethany woke up just as the burning house collapsed.

It was a horrible dream, one that left her pulse hammering like a drumbeat. Blazing birthday cakes aside, it also made her feel as if she'd missed something important, a sign. Her mind returned to the image of Nate standing at the end of the table, standing apart from the others, watching her, his dark eyes shining as she lit the candles. She lingered on him. It was the only bright spot in an otherwise morbid dream.

Bethany swung her feet over the side of the bed and touched the cold wood floor. She slipped into her flip-flops, threw on her long sweater, and crossed the small space to press the switch on the coffeemaker. Soon, the comforting hiss of coffee brewing filled her room.

She picked up her phone and checked for messages.

Nothing.

She pressed her lips together, frustrated with herself when she realized why she was disappointed.

Bethany set the phone down. "You do not want him to be your next ex-boyfriend. Trust me," she said aloud. She poured herself some coffee, sipping it and letting the steam wash over her face. The Red Hot Gala tickets Darcy had given her lay next to the pot. They couldn't be more ostentatious, gaudy metallic gold and red paper with glitter hearts popping out all over the invite. She picked up one and studied it, then slapped it down again. She didn't want to think about that now.

Nate had yet to call about seeing her again. He'd made such a point of teasing her about what they'd do, but her phone remained annoyingly silent. She brought her coffee and phone over to the couch and sank into the soft folds. She stared at the black screen, willing it to light up.

What was wrong with her? What was it about him that caused this restless energy? She couldn't remember the last time she wanted someone to call her this badly, and it made her a little angry. Gran liked to remind her that appearing desperate was no good. "Never run after a bus or a man," she liked to say. "Another one will eventually come along." Dear Gran. Bethany bet she was a firecracker before she met Grandpa Joe.

Frustrated, she tossed the phone to the end of the couch where it bounced off a throw pillow and thumped onto the floor. Running her fingers through her hair, Bethany leaned back and looked at the ceiling. Nate's appeal must be wrapped up in the fact that he traveled. She'd always dated local guys from Hendricks, Dentsen, or Two Rivers, and once in a while she'd meet someone in town who lived in Silma or Bonville, an hour up Highway 61. Bethany knew she'd run into them before long if they didn't call. But they always did. Nate lived and worked in Duluth and traveled for his freelance work. That must be the appeal. Nate wasn't permanent. He simply wouldn't be around forever, so they already had a built-in breakup in the near future. But she liked him. The fact was, she probably would have kept him around a little longer if it was under her control. That was the difference between Nate and the others.

Bethany felt better already now that she understood her irritability. She'd call him to tell him she enjoyed the dinner, which wasn't needy at all but grateful. Then she'd mention the Red Hot Gala tickets and—

No.

She'd wait for his call. His number would show on her phone's display by the end of the day, she was sure of it. She wouldn't get too involved with him and only agree to one more date. The Red Hot Gala was out of the question. She'd take Ethan instead.

Bethany lounged there for ten minutes, going over the details of their dinner date in her mind again like she'd done for the last few days, and she almost pitched herself over the arm of the couch when her phone buzzed from its position on the floor.

She scooped it up and pressed the touch screen. "Hello?"

It was Nate.

"I'm in the neighborhood. Care if I stop by?" His husky voice sounded even deeper over the phone.

"Your grandmother's house is two blocks away. You're *always* in the neighborhood."

"Is that a 'yes'?"

She crossed her ankles on the arm of her futon, grinning. "I wouldn't be very neighborly if I said you couldn't, right?"

"I'll be right there."

Bethany jumped to her feet. "Give me three minutes."

She spent that time throwing the comforter over her bed, whipping her hair into shape with a comb and a little spray, and shucking the threadbare cover-up for a clean, oversized sweater. She smoothed the fabric over her stomach as she pulled open the door. Nate closed the garden gate behind him and followed the brick path to her house, all swagger and smiles.

Bethany winced as he ducked to avoid hitting his forehead on her wind chimes.

"Hi there," he said, walking past her into the house as she held the door open.

"Hi yourself."

She silently scolded herself after hearing the sound of her own voice. Purring wouldn't be an inaccurate way to describe it. *Don't be ridiculous, Bethany*. He had that same rakish quality that made Robert Downey, Jr. so attractive, though—the unkempt hair, soulful eyes, and the self-deprecating humor that got Bethany every time. But she was *not* the swooning type. Gran scoffed at such foolishness and had schooled Bethany on behaving herself around men. Bethany lifted her arm toward the inside. "Come in."

He looked over his shoulder toward Gran's house. "This isn't forbidden, is it? Allowing male guests inside your house?"

"Are you joking?" She regretted how that sounded. "Gran installed a camera in here ages ago. Nothing that goes on in here will go unnoticed."

Nate froze mid-stride, his mouth half opened, like a beached fish gasping for air.

Bethany couldn't help herself. "I'm kidding!"

He exhaled loudly. "Oh man. That about did me in."

"You're an easy mark." She led him inside, picking up an overlooked sock hanging over the back of her armchair and stuffed it into her sweater's pocket. "I wouldn't put it past her, though. She can be a little ornery."

He chuckled. "I'll have to meet her."

When Bethany didn't respond, he rubbed his hands together. "I meant to call earlier, but I got busy with the house. Organizing a lifetime of stuff takes more time than you think."

"I can't even imagine." At her kitchen counter, she lifted the coffee pot. "Want some coffee?"

He came closer. "No, thanks. I didn't even intend to stop, but I was going past and—"

"And what?"

"About that date."

She leaned against the counter. "The one where I'm supposed to wear some subarctic outfit so I don't turn into a human popsicle?"

He smiled. "Yes, that one. Saturday night okay?"

She rolled her eyes but kept smiling. "I suppose."

"You won't regret it."

"I'm intrigued."

Nate's shoulders relaxed. He glanced around her studio. "Nice place."

"Thanks. It's home sweet home."

He walked over to the shelf in the corner that held the pottery her Gran had made years ago, and a few prized ceramic pieces too.

"My grandmother worked with ceramics," Nate said, his

voice trailing off. He picked one up and studied the bottom. "Nineteen eighty-nine. H.M.S. What's that?"

"Handmakery Studio. That's the folk arts school in Dentsen. Who knows, they probably took a class together."

He replaced the pot and picked up a bird sculpture, one of her favorite pieces.

"She didn't make that, but I love it anyway. Gran gave it to me when I was little."

Nate turned it over too. "Interesting," he mused, before setting it back in its place. He came toward her again and was about to say something else, but his gaze fell to the counter where the two Gala tickets lay, and by the time it registered with Bethany what caught his eye, it was too late to push them under the stack of nearby bills.

Nate's eyebrows shot up. "Red Hot Gala. Now that sounds like a good time."

Bethany shrugged. "Eh. It's just a benefit. Happens every year. I probably won't go." *Why didn't she think to hide them?*

"But you have tickets."

"My friend Darcy gave them to me. She manages the venue." She didn't want to make eye contact.

Nate shifted his weight. "What's the organization?"

"Sorry?"

"You said it was a benefit."

Bethany's face flushed. What was the organization? Her brain turned to oatmeal. "It...It's for the Broman County Arts Guild."

His gaze held hers. "I see."

An awkward silence wrapped around them. He didn't seem ready to leave. Bethany wasn't sure where their conversation was headed until she blurted out, "Do you want to go?"

"I'd love to."

What had she just done?

"But will you still be in Hendricks on—" she fumbled for one of the tickets, squinting at the date— "February eighth? Maybe that's looking ahead too far."

Nate straightened. He wore an amused grin. "I might be back in Duluth at that point, but I can certainly come back for it."

Bethany put her hand up. "No, my mistake. I thought you said you'd be around for another month."

"It's just two hours away. It's no trouble at all."

She almost clapped her hand to her forehead in frustration. He didn't sound like he'd take "no" for an answer. "Really. We don't have to go. Like I said, I was actually thinking about skipping it."

Nate pressed his palms together pleadingly. "I'd love to come. I'm serious."

Bethany looked down at her bare feet, gritting her teeth. What made her ask him to the Red Hot Gala after telling herself she didn't want to go?

She forced a smile. "Okay then. It's a date." She couldn't back out now. Nate looked so *eager*.

"Great. If anything, I'm looking forward to seeing if I recognize anyone." He backed toward the door. "I'll take off since I barged in on your quiet morning in the first place." Bethany swore his voice sounded a little uneven. "And about Saturday. Is seven o'clock okay?"

"That's fine. I'll see you then." She put one hand on the

doorknob. *Just go, please.*

Bethany chewed on her lip as she watched him follow the brick path through the gate again. What happened to letting this union between her and Nate run its course, and asking Ethan, good ol' safe Ethan, to the Gala instead? Her once reasonable head had betrayed her. Bethany scratched the area behind her ear that turned itchy when she was put on the spot. What a mess she'd got herself into this morning and she hadn't even been awake an hour. Two dates with Nate Ransom when just twenty minutes ago she willed herself to let their association die a natural death.

Bethany was still in a whirl of panic as she drove along Highway 61 to Blueberry Point Lodge. With no classes scheduled for the day, Bethany promised Darcy she'd help her formulate a decorating plan for the gala. They'd spend the morning poring over ideas they found online while sitting on the plush red couch that Bethany promised would go missing someday when Darcy wasn't looking. It was Bethany's favorite piece of furniture in the whole inn. She'd immerse herself in choosing centerpieces and mood lighting and forget about how her cool demeanor seemed to go up in flames when Nate appeared.

The tiled roof of Blueberry Point Lodge came into view above the trees. Bethany turned into the gravel drive, following it past the expansive lawn, and toward the mansion with pillars and windows galore. As a little girl, she dreamed she lived there in the sandstone castle with a barn full of dragons as pets and a couple of princes from distant kingdoms who traveled day and night for a kiss. Bethany grimaced at the memory as she pulled under the massive carport and turned off the ignition. Princes, indeed. Bethany shut her car door and bounded up the stone steps, not bothering to ring the bell. Darcy knew she was coming.

She marveled at Darcy's luck in getting to stay on at the inn to manage it for the new owners, the Stetmans of Sturgeon Widows Tours. They were expanding their tour business to include the inn to host guests for overnight stays. For Darcy it was a seamless transition, having worked for the previous owners of the inn, Ingrid and Henry Callahan, before they sold the house last fall due to Henry's poor health. Darcy's good fortune might have something to do with Sean Stetman being crazy about her, but Darcy's work ethic was long established before she and Sean started dating.

Bethany walked inside the foyer to find Darcy already in the living room with her laptop, her curls piled high on her head in a messy knot, lounging in pajama pants on the couch.

"Don't get too close. I'm coming down with something," Darcy said, dabbing at her nose with a tissue.

"We could have postponed." Bethany brushed a tissue off the cushion on the far end of the couch before she sat down.

Darcy waved her tissue. "Not necessary. I'll just aim my sneezes the other way. Besides, I'm planning to have this cold two days and that's it."

Bethany kicked off her shoes. "Good luck with that." She paused. "Is Sean taking care of you?"

Darcy winced. "When he isn't catering to Paige and her photo shoot of the inn and tour building," she said in a whisper.

"She's here? Now?"

Darcy pointed upstairs, a wry smile on her face. "I think he's more upset than I am."

"That's not saying much. You don't look very upset."

"Sean acts as if the situation is way worse than it is. It's not as if she's come back to resume their relationship."

"Yes, but she really did a number on him from what you told me."

"I know. I'm trying to be sensitive to it."

Bethany leaned back against the couch. "I have to meet this one. She sounds like more trouble than I am."

"Don't be silly. You don't make ridiculous demands of people like she did with Sean."

"No, I just pretend they don't exist. One day we're dating, the next day we're not."

Darcy sniffled into yet another tissue. "Clean breaks are better than months-long drama."

Bethany put her feet up on the coffee table and opened her laptop. For the next several minutes, she and Darcy searched party decor sites, speaking in hushed tones, hoping to catch the sound of footfalls before Sean and Paige appeared.

"What about the color scheme?" asked Darcy, tapping the end of her pen to her lips. "Should it match the invites? I shouldn't have procrastinated this long. This could have been done weeks ago."

"Relax. That's why I'm here. Let's go for gold and red

with touches of black. Elegant. Not too garish. And it will match my dress."

Darcy threw her head back, laughing. "That figures."

"What?"

"That you'd choose the decor around your outfit."

"I thought everyone did that?"

Darcy gave her a sidelong glance. "Not everyone."

A few minutes of silence passed while they looked at idea boards.

Bethany sighed. "So I asked him."

Darcy gasped. "Nate what's-his-name? What did he say?"

"What I expected he'd say. That he'll have moved back to Duluth by then, but he'll come back to go with me."

"Of course he would."

"That's the problem. He's too accommodating. He'll probably realize that as soon as he moves back to Duluth. And then he'll feel obligated—"

Darcy pursed her lips. "You're imagining a problem when there isn't one."

Voices from the kitchen drifted into the living room.

Darcy glanced at her wide-eyed and grimaced. Bethany rubbed her hands together, zeroing in on the kitchen door.

Darcy swatted her in the arm. "Don't look so bloodthirsty."

"Who? Me?" Bethany lowered her voice. "I don't have a reason to—"

Sean came through the swinging doors then, and the look on his face almost made Bethany burst out laughing. He wasn't one for pretending, but he could really use a little discretion in showing his feelings. Bethany could almost see the roiling thundercloud over his head.

"Hey, Sean." Bethany mustered up her cheeriest smile.

One corner of his mouth twitched upward.

Darcy set her laptop on the table and got up. "Guess who Bethany's bringing to the Gala? Do you remember Nate Ransom? He moved away in junior high."

"Anyone who was under five feet tall remembered him. He was Goliath."

"Still is," Bethany said, wiggling her eyebrows at Darcy.

"Bethany, this is Paige Goff," Sean said in a monotone. "Paige is a photographer on a magazine assignment."

Paige extended her hand to Bethany, her grip solid, almost painful. "Pleasure," Paige said.

Bethany dropped her hand behind her back, flexing the pain away. In an instant, she knew exactly why Sean resented his former girlfriend. Sometimes the look on a person's face can sum up their whole character, and that's how Bethany knew Paige was a stubborn and prideful adversary, owning more than her fair share of spite when life didn't go her way. Maybe it was the angle of her square chin when she lifted it ever so slightly to look at Bethany. Or the set of her lips when someone spoke, like she wasn't taking them seriously. Whatever it was, Bethany knew that she didn't have much to say to Paige Goff.

Ever the hostess, Darcy offered to have lunch delivered from Red's Tavern if Paige wanted to stay, much to Sean's horror, who shook his head vigorously behind Paige's back.

Paige gathered the dark curtain of hair hanging freely

down her back and twisted it over her shoulder, a showy display if Bethany ever saw one.

"I need to get back to the hotel and see if I have anything worth using from this morning," Paige said, hoisting the camera slung around her neck. Her forced smile only grew more rigid as she looked at Darcy. "But thank you." Then she turned to Sean. "Take me back?"

"I'll get my keys," he said under his breath.

"Great. I'll follow." She held out both hands to Darcy, who had folded herself onto the couch again, surrounded by tissues.

Darcy crossed her arms, sticking her hands into her armpits. "It would probably be better if we didn't touch."

"You're right," she said, and clutched her balled fists against her chest in a hurry. "And thanks for letting me borrow Sean this morning."

Sean came forward and leaned over Darcy, whispering something in her ear. Bethany didn't miss the soft look he gave her as Darcy laughed at their secret. Nor did she miss how Paige leaned closer, trying to catch Sean's words. Her eyes narrowed momentarily at their intimate exchange, and Bethany would have missed it if she hadn't been watching for the woman's reaction.

If Paige didn't leave in a hurry, Bethany wouldn't be able to hold back a comment or two. The woman was as sincere as Silda when the sneaky thing pretended to spare the birds and mice she toyed with in Gran's backyard. Bethany couldn't stand that about her cat, how Silda released them so the poor animals could scamper to safety, only to be knocked down again seconds before their escape.

Paige swept her hair over her other shoulder. She glanced at Bethany as she backed toward the door. "I've forgotten your—"

Bethany wiggled her fingers at Paige. "Pleasure."

Paige's thin-lipped smile wavered. "Yes."

As Bethany and Darcy sat silently as they left, Darcy glanced at her as if to say, *she's something, isn't she?*

Bethany responded with a look toward the ceiling as if to say, *this room isn't big enough for all of us.*

When the front door clicked close, Bethany heaved an exaggerated sigh. "My word, that woman is full of herself."

"I know! I don't think Sean told her we're dating. If there was any doubt, it's gone now."

"Definitely. People like her are master manipulators. I'm sure she'll get the details from him somehow. Better watch yourself."

Darcy hitched a shoulder. "Let her think what she wants. She's not my problem."

"True. I don't think Sean's dislike could have been written any more clear on his face." Bethany tried to imitate Sean's expression but couldn't keep a straight face.

Darcy shook her head, laughing. "I need to talk with him about that. She's promoting the company after all. He could stand to be a little nicer."

Bethany scoffed. "You're much more patient than I am."

"We won't be seeing her for much longer. Besides, getting this place in order is my first priority. The sooner we can start hosting guests overnight, the sooner my routine will return to normal."

"And the sooner you can start planning your wedding."

Bethany snuck a glance at Darcy.

"My wedding?! I think you're forgetting we're not even engaged."

"Yet."

Darcy's smile suggested that she'd thought about the possibility.

Bethany closed her laptop. "I envy you."

Darcy's smile disappeared. "Why?"

"Because you have a good guy who adores you. Your future is set."

"I don't know about the 'set' part," Darcy said, shifting on the couch so she could see Bethany squarely. "You can have that, too, you know."

She couldn't imagine. Bethany shuddered.

"But first of all, you have to be open to it. That means no set limits on the amount of time you spend dating one guy. Give this Nate guy a chance."

Bethany pressed her lips together and set the laptop on the table. "I might if he didn't live in Duluth. I'm not up for long-distance relationships."

Darcy rolled her eyes. "There you go again."

"What?"

"Ending it before it begins."

"I have a chronic problem, don't I?"

Darcy nodded absently and blew her nose in response.

Bethany crossed her ankles on the tabletop again. Maybe that should have been a New Year's resolution too. *Don't throw away a relationship before it has a chance.*

She'd work on that resolution with the next guy who didn't live two hours away.

Chapter Eight

On Saturday night at five minutes to seven o'clock, Nate left his driveway amid a soft snowfall. His grandmother's house was two blocks from Bethany's place, in a neighborhood dotted with Cape Cod-style houses and tidy ranches. Christmas lights strung across front porches and wrapped around landscaping resembled any small town in America, and he'd been to plenty. Most of them didn't have the Big Lake as a backdrop though, now invisible in the inky darkness, a few blocks south down Water Street, like a silent, watchful presence.

Against the nagging voice in his head that told him she might not enjoy tonight as much as he hoped, he'd cut a hole in the ice near Clearwater Lighthouse earlier while the day was still light and set up his shelter. The temperature reading on his dashboard now told him it was twenty-three degrees, not very cold by his standards, but his needs weren't the issue. He'd had to get creative to make sure Bethany was comfortable.

Nate knew he had to walk a fine line with her. Bethany was skittish for whatever reason. If he overplayed his hand, overwhelmed her with too much too fast, she'd disappear. It was his weakness, the over-the-top gestures. Jana liked to tease him that he scared them off because he was too nice. Whatever *that* meant.

When Nate pulled up to her grandmother's house, Bethany again met him at her gate, as if she wanted to avoid him coming to her door. They drove for ten minutes along Highway 61, talking about a freelance assignment he hoped to get, one that would take him to California, and about what compelled her to open a yoga studio. Before long, he stopped the Rover. The light atop Clearwater Lighthouse flashed intermittently.

She looked through the windshield and out her side window. "Where are we, Nate?"

"At Clearwater Beach. See?" He pointed in the general direction of where he thought he'd set up the ice fishing shelter. "There's the lighthouse."

"That was a rhetorical question. I meant *what* are we doing here?"

"We're fishing."

She turned in her seat to look at him squarely. "*Ice-fishing?*"

He could make out a hint of a smile on her face from the glow of the dashboard lights, and struggled to keep his own expression neutral.

"Well, I don't think we'll be able to get a line in the lake as is so, yes, ice-fishing."

Bethany blew air out of her mouth in a short, fast burst which made him chuckle. "There is no way I'm getting out of this car, slipping across the ice, to sit in a tent and stare at a hole in the lake."

"Phrasing it that way, it does sound pretty ridiculous." Self-doubt reared its head a little higher.

"You said 'picnic.' How is ice-fishing a picnic?"

"This is a compromise. You were worried about being cold so I put up the shelter and brought some blankets."

"On the other hand, you did come to yoga class, a class full of women—

"I didn't see that as a negative really."

"—so I guess I can endure a few minutes of this."

"There you go. I knew you'd be game."

"I'm game for fifteen minutes, Ransom. You're on the clock."

His hand was on the door handle. "Let's not waste time then."

She met him at the front of the Rover so Nate could take her arm and help her walk through the layer of fresh snow that had fallen in the last two hours. Of course her choice of footwear leaned more toward fashionable than fishable. She didn't take him seriously when he told her to dress warm. The lighthouse loomed ahead of them, its beacon enticing them ahead toward the dark, frozen lake.

"Look straight ahead, past the lighthouse. See it?" Nate drew Bethany close, touching heads, as he pointed. A dim light fifty yards away illuminated a small white tent.

Bethany giggled. "That's cuter than I thought it'd be. Kind of charming actually."

"I knew you'd like it." Reluctantly, he stepped back.

She nudged him gently in the ribs. "Don't get too cocky. I'm still basking in the heat from your air vents. Twenty more steps and you'll wish you never met me."

"You don't scare me, Marconi. I've met worse."

Again she laughed, causing her foot to slip slightly. Nate caught her elbow and steadied her.

"Wait until I break something on this ice. Then you'll think twice about that."

"Empty threats, all of them." He clutched her arm tighter and circled his other around the vicinity of her hips, hard to tell in her bulky coat. Nate wished it was a little farther between where they stood and the lighthouse.

"So I'm assuming there's a path out to that igloo of discomfort?"

"Of course. It's already taken care of."

"And there's a hot beverage waiting for me?"

"It's probably not hot anymore, but it will definitely warm you up."

Her hair brushed his cheek when she turned toward him again. "You did think of everything. I'm impressed."

"You have no idea. Now stop asking questions before I give away all my surprises."

"Unquenchable inquisitiveness is part of my DNA. Whoa, say that five times. Unquenchable inqu—"

"Let's get into the shack first then we can have the contest."

They followed the path on the ice that Nate shoveled

from shore to the shack. As they drew closer, Bethany lifted her nose slightly.

"Do I smell...cookies? Have you been baking in there?"

He laughed. "Now that would be something. Get inside before your feet get frostbit in those shoes."

Nate swept aside the canvas door and let her enter. He wished he could see her face except she was in front of him. A few seconds later, her reaction made up for what he missed.

"Is this for real? I feel like I'm on a movie set," she said, stroking the plush folding chair, marveling at the battery-powered string lights hanging around the top of the tent. Nate spent a fortune on them after Jana suggested dressing up the shelter. It needs ambience, his sister had reasoned.

Nate stuffed his hands in his coat pockets and watched the smile dance across her features. She was a snow angel, dressed head to toe in cream and white, from the faux fur-lined aviator hat to her mukluks. The only contrasting color were her eyes, which reminded him of his grandmother's blue Depression glass.

"Do you like it?"

"Like it? I want to live here," she said, her gaze wandering around the space, picking up the details Nate planned with Jana's help: the cookie-scented candle, the thermos of hot chocolate, and the fishing rod he'd bought for her just yesterday.

Nate lifted the thermos next to his chair and poured her a drink.

"Did anyone see you cart all of this stuff out here? I bet

it took you a few trips." She held the cup between her mittened hands and lifted it to her lips.

He tightened the lid on the thermos. "Herschel Whittaker saw me haul out the initial load when I pulled up to the lighthouse. He didn't have any visitors, so he helped me make the second trip."

Nate set the cooler on his legs, opening the lid. He took each item out and held it up. "Let's see: turkey wrap, apple salad, and for dessert, ginger cookies."

"Did you make all that?"

"Only the cookies. The deli bar takes credit for the wrap and salad."

"This reminds me that I skipped lunch. Can we eat?"

"You're the boss. I can't very well deny you food since I dragged you out here."

So Nate finished unpacking the cooler, and they ate in relative silence for a while until she told him the story about how she'd almost gone ice fishing once with Gran and one of the men Gran dated after Grandpa Joe passed away. But Bethany didn't like him, so she played sick and caused Gran to cancel the date.

"Conniving," Nate mused.

Bethany's eyes grew wide. "You have no idea. Gran says I was quite the pill."

The air inside the shelter had grown warm and Bethany unzipped her coat halfway. "We're not going to melt the ice and fall through, are we? I mean, it's a lot more warm in here than it is out there."

"That depends on how fast it heats up."

"Maybe I should stop talking so much," she said with a half smile.

Nate chuckled. "You said it. I didn't."

"I'm truly impressed." Her gaze rested on him. "Thank you, Nate. I love this."

Nate flushed at the compliment and looked away. Suddenly, he was the awkward pre-teen who was just noticed by the prettiest, most popular girl in school. Words escaped him, and he only managed to mumble "you're welcome" before he gathered the empty wrappers, stuffing them back into the cooler. Then he grabbed both poles in the corner where they rested in holders. He held one out to her.

Bethany set her mug down. "Confession: I've never fished before," she said, reaching for it and gripping the pole like it was a foreign object. "Well, technically I did when I was a kid, but I don't count it because it seems like another lifetime.

Nate moved his chair closest to hers. Holding her hands while she clutched the pole, Nate checked the reel then dropped the line into the round, dark hole he'd cut into the ice that afternoon. "Nothing to it really. Wait for a tug."

She sank farther into the chair, a content look on her face. Nate scooped up the fleece blanket behind him and draped it over her shoulders. He watched her from above for a few seconds and wished he could sit and look at her for a bit longer without being obvious. Instead, he settled in his own seat and kept an eye on her line.

"Why did you come to see me?"

When Nate looked at Bethany, he found her studying him, her head tilted to one side, a lazy smile on her lips.

"What do you mean?"

Her gaze returned to the hole in the ice. "Well, we weren't exactly friends in school. And then you moved away."

"I guess I just wanted to connect with someone from school. No one lives here anymore."

"So I'm the consolation prize. The last resort."

He chuckled. "Why do you do that?"

"Do what?"

"Talk so negatively about yourself. Think the worst."

Bethany waved her hand. "That's a conversation for another day."

"You've said that before too."

"I did?"

"Yeah. So maybe today should be the day to have that conversation. I'd like to hear it."

"I can't sit in this little slice of heaven you worked so hard to make and ruin the night with my tales of woe."

"You couldn't possibly ruin my night, Bethany."

She smiled slightly before her gaze dropped to her lap. He thought she was avoiding the topic again until she cleared her throat.

"First, a disclaimer," she said. "Gran is the woman of the century. What she had to go through with my grandfather's death and then putting up with me as a teenager amazes me."

Nate chuckled. "I don't doubt that she's an exceptional

woman. Look at you, after all. You're pretty accomplished yourself."

"Your sense of humor is in top form—"

He held his hand up. "If you're going to cut yourself down every time I try to give you a compliment tonight, I'm going to use you as bait on the end of this line."

Bethany threw back her head and laughed. "You wouldn't dare."

"Try me."

"You'll need to cut a bigger hole."

"You're stalling."

"Fine." She sighed. "I told you my parents worked away from home during the week when I was younger. They're attorneys in Minneapolis."

"Go on."

"I realized early on that I didn't have the typical...family life. Since my grandma showed up for most of my school events and ballet recitals, kids in school sometimes asked why my parents never came. I used to make up these wild stories about them. They were on a jungle safari, they were scientists in Antarctica or on a mission trip in Mozambique."

"Basically, a reason why they weren't where you thought they should be."

"Yes." Bethany's voice grew quiet. "I was embarrassed, angry, and confused about why I couldn't have normal parents who came home every night."

"That's understandable."

"And then I started to believe it was my fault."

"Why?"

"I thought they didn't want to live in Hendricks or move me to Minneapolis with them," she said, jiggling her pole a little. "I feel something. Do I have a fish?"

The tip of the pole bent downward. Bethany stood up, eyes wide. "What do I do?"

"Turn the reel towards you."

She gritted her teeth, looking between him and the pole. "I don't think I can do this."

He grinned at the delight on her face. "Sure you can."

Bethany inched around the hole toward him, trying to pass him the pole. "Here. You do it."

Nate leaned away from her, chuckling. "No way. This is your victory."

"But I'm going to fall in or something."

"I guarantee you're not going to fall into that tiny hole. I'm curious to know what the 'or something' might entail though." He moved the cooler out of the way so she wouldn't trip over it. "You might want to bring the pole up as your reeling. That ensures the hook catches."

She jerked the pole toward the ceiling a little too fast, though, and would have tumbled backward over her chair if it wasn't for Nate's quick reflexes. He sent his own chair flying in the effort to catch her from falling, and managed to hook one arm around her to keep her upright. Nate pulled her closer to regain his balance lest they both tumble over backward. He was acutely aware of how close their bodies pressed together and he stalled a few extra seconds before he released her.

Bethany straightened her hat. "Whoa—close one!" she said.

Nate picked up the pole beside them on the ice. The line was slack. He held is up to Bethany who noted the lack of activity now and did an admirable job of looking disappointed.

"That's too bad," she said. "Maybe next time."

"You're no actress."

She threw her hands on her waist. "Wait—what?"

"I'd bet my parka right now that you're relieved there's no fish on the end of this line."

Her eyes sparked in the lantern light as she tried to keep a straight face. "I'm completely ruined. I used every ounce of my patience to hook that stupid thing."

"That's a fish story if I ever heard one."

Bethany stepped up to him. She poked him in the chest as she looked into his eyes, the defiant tilt to her chin daring him to come closer. Nate planted his feet and willed them not to move an inch. He didn't think either of them were ready for what he had in mind.

"Someday I'm going to out fish you, Nate Ransom."

Someday.

Nate was acutely aware of the pounding in his chest. He was sure she could hear it too.

Someday.

That sounded more long-term than a date or two during the next month. She must have realized what her words implied too, because she leaned back slightly to study his face.

"That sounds like a challenge," he said in a hushed tone. His voice came from somewhere else, like he was outside of the shelter in the dark, frosty night.

"That it is," she whispered, looking at his lips.

For a few frozen moments, Nate thought about kissing her. Her mouth opened slightly like she expected him to, but then a shout from outside broke the spell. Bethany startled.

"Hello?"

The voice was closer.

"I recognize that voice," Bethany said, her hand still on her chest.

"Everything all right in there?"

"Bernie Rehm?" Bethany called. She looked at Nate. "He's a cop here in town. Good guy," she whispered. "Yes, we're fine, Bernie. It's me. Bethany. Come on in here." She unzipped the opening and stepped aside.

Seconds later, the man's meaty face poked through the opening. His brown hat and bottle brush mustache sported snowflakes, a sign that the forecast had been correct: there were a few more inches of snow on the way.

"I was doing my rounds in the lighthouse parking lot and saw your shadows. It looked like you guys were fighting or something."

Nate laughed. "Or something. Bethany hooked a fish." He extended his hand. "Nate Ransom."

The officer shook Nate's hand but his eyes kept roving the shelter. "Whoa. This is some setup. I guess you two aren't just here to catch supper, are you?" He winked at Nate.

Bethany ignored him. "But it got away," she said. "Gran never taught me how to fish."

Bernie stepped farther into the shelter, his eyes taking in

the overturned chair, the forlorn pole leaning against the wall, the mug laying on its side, a pool of hot chocolate seeping into the ice floor. He was almost as tall as Nate and twice as wide.

"That surprises me," Bernie said, his focus back on Nate and Bethany. "If anything, I'd count on Donna to teach her granddaughter how to be self-sufficient. Why, it wasn't too long ago that I got a lecture because my five-year-old grandson couldn't start a fire when she was with the Kiwanis group at the park."

Bethany shook her head. "That sounds like Gran."

Bernie pointed at Nate. "So your name's Ransom? You related to Marcine Ransom?"

"She was my grandmother."

"Heck of a lady," he said. Bernie backed toward the doorway. "I won't keep you any longer as long as you two are okay. Gotta check things out."

"We appreciate that, Bernie," she said. "There's nothing wrong here except my bruised ego."

The man gave one last look around before he stepped out of the tent. Bethany closed it behind him.

She turned to Nate, leaning close so Bernie didn't hear, even though he was probably halfway to his cruiser by now.

"I'd bet anything he was hoping to catch someone making out or something. He's a big gossip." She straightened her hat that was still askew from tussling with the pole. Her blonde hair spilled from beneath it. She glanced at him, and Nate sensed she was looking for his reaction.

As a newspaper reporter, Nate and his cool demeanor

were well practiced. It came in handy during interviews, and especially in his early days as a writer fresh out of college and stuck with the less-than-desirable assignments. Talking to irate parents after school board meetings and witnesses at crime scenes took steel-wrapped nerves at times, and the less emotion he showed, the better. But while his expression remained unaffected, underneath the surface was a different story. Antacids were his best friends in those days. And he was especially thankful for his composure now in this enclosed space with Bethany, who seemed to enjoy referencing a scenario that he'd only daydreamed about until now.

"Nah. He was just doing his job."

Bethany raised her eyebrows. "You're naive."

Nate snorted. "No. Just giving the poor guy the benefit of the doubt."

She shrugged off the idea, apparently growing bored with the direction their conversation took. Bethany picked up her pole, then wheeled around.

"Wait a minute. I thought I started this conversation by asking why you came to see me. And you never answered."

"Yes, I did. I said I wanted to connect with someone from school." Nate sat in his chair.

She stared at him sideways, pressing her lips together. "I don't believe you," she said finally.

Nate leaned back and hooked his fingers together behind his head. "Okay. Why don't you tell me why I came to see you. You seem to have all the answers."

The air stretched tight between them. Again, she smiled at him in a way that suggested she was weighing her answers. "I have my suspicions. But I'm going to wait before I give you a definite answer."

"I'll be on the edge of my seat until then."

Their eyes locked long enough that Nate held his breath, waiting to see if she'd be the first one to look away.

A few seconds later, she did. A shadow crossed her face as she pulled her collar tighter around her neck. "Maybe we should go. The snow looked like it was coming down heavier when Bernie left."

"You want to leave already?" He sat up, studying her. Disappointment seeped into his bones. Hadn't they been flirting seconds ago? Was it something he said? Or didn't say? "You didn't even finish your story about your parents."

"It's nothing." Bethany's indifferent expression spoke volumes. She checked the time on her phone.

"Did I…do something?"

Bethany hesitated. "I just don't want to get snowed in out here," she said, her attention on the mittens that she slipped back onto her hands.

Nate sighed. "Yes, you're probably right."

It didn't take long to gather up their chairs, poles, and the decorations that Nate had spent hours buying and setting up. He wondered if his efforts were worth it. Ambience was expensive and time consuming, and it seemed Bethany couldn't care less about the trouble he took to make the night special. He'd be sure to ask Jana what he should do with yards of battery-powered string lights now.

With Bethany's help, the shelter came down in a hurry too. They worked silently. Together they made several trips to the Rover, stuffing all of the supplies into the back. Her hair wet with melted snow, Bethany sat next to him, lost in thought on the drive to her place. When he pulled up alongside the fence outside of her studio, Bethany flashed him a quick smile and a hurried thanks but was gone before he could say good night.

The night didn't end as he'd hoped. Truthfully, Nate didn't really have any expectations other than getting to know her better, but he couldn't help feeling they'd parted on a less-than-ideal note. Something turned Bethany's mood sour and he had no idea what did it.

He drove home wondering how the night would have turned out if it weren't for Bernie the cop.

Chapter Nine

Bethany spent much of the day tallying reasons why she should back out of taking Nate to the Red Hot Gala. She'd even jotted down a con list by rewriting all her pro points as negatives.

Too polite.

Too confident.

Way too good-looking.

Too accommodating.

She'd been so involved in turning his good traits into faults that she forgot about the one detail she'd been clinging to all along: he lived too far away.

Bethany simply couldn't get involved with him; she'd wasted enough time already thinking about him, talking to him, trying to ignore her attraction to him when she knew with certainty that her heart would eventually be broken.

Saturday night had been magical. Nate proved himself to be deserving of someone who loved to be spoiled. He'd obviously put much thought into her ice-fishing experience. And yes, she enjoyed every minute of it, but...

Bethany growled under her breath. The "buts" always stopped her cold. For every nice guy she dated, a string of "buts" always doomed the relationship. And this time Nate seemed the nicest guy by far. All the more reason to call it quits before her heart suffered for her muddled thinking.

After her three o'clock meditation class, Bethany intended to go straight home, but she turned on Water Street, climbing the hill toward the last houses on the road. Marcine Ransom's house was on the right side, a good-sized Cape Cod with an enormous white pine in the front yard and a wooden yellow bench on the front porch. No curtains covered the picture window, so her visit wouldn't be a surprise if he happened to see her pull into the drive.

She'd level with Nate once and for all.

On the porch, a piece of duct tape covered a hole where the doorbell should have been, so Bethany knocked twice on the door.

No answer.

She knocked again.

This time a female voice shouted, followed by rumbling and crashing from some point farther in the house. Seconds later, the lock clicked and the door flew open. A petite young woman stood there, one hand on her hip, looking harried and pleasantly surprised at the same time.

Bethany took a step back, surprised herself. She expected Nate at the door.

"Bethany, right?" The woman's brows arched in

expectation. She stuck out her hand. "I'm Jana, Nate's sister."

Of course she was. Jana shared the same dark eyes and thin, regal nose.

"Yes, I'm Bethany. It's nice to meet you. Is Nate here?" She peered over Jana's shoulder into the living room that was stacked with boxes in all corners of the room. Music played somewhere inside the house, a mellow, bluesy sound.

Jana stepped aside. "Come in before you freeze. Yes, he's here. Nate's probably just too lazy to get off the floor or something." Her expression told Bethany that, to Jana, Nate's laziness was a recurring problem.

"Nate!"

Jana's surprisingly robust voice carried throughout the house.

"He gets involved with sorting through our grandmother's stuff and next thing you know, two hours have passed and all he's accomplished is reading a box full of old letters."

In one of the back rooms, the music stopped. More stumbling over large objects. Footsteps drew closer.

"You're bellowing like a cow. What for?" he grumbled in the hall, still out of sight.

Then he came around the corner and froze. His expression was comical, saucer-eyed and slack-mouthed. Jana thought so too. She snorted.

"You have company," Jana said.

Nate's surprise turned into obvious delight. He shucked the grimy dust rag draped over one shoulder.

"Bethany." He paused, his eyes darting from her to his sister. "You two met?"

Jana tapped him playfully on the shoulder. "Of course. I introduced myself when I answered the door since you're once again in outer space." She turned to Bethany. "He's about as lazy as a junior high student with a weekend supply of chips and drinks and a gaming system at their fingertips."

Nate shook his head abruptly, grinning. "Lies as usual. She likes to paint me as the monster older brother."

Bethany couldn't help smiling at their sibling banter.

"I shouldn't have popped over without calling. You two are obviously busy—"

"Nonsense," Nate said. "I was about ready for a break." He ignored Jana, whose fingers pressed against her lips to contain her laughter.

Bethany followed Nate into the dining room, a bright, airy room, despite the heavy furniture—an ornately carved dining table, its matching chairs, and a sideboard. The pieces reminded Bethany of an old English manor house. Unlike the living room, the dining area hadn't been dismantled yet. Nate pulled out a chair for her to sit down, but she walked to the sliding door leading to a quaint wooden deck instead. Beyond the deck, the yard pressed against the encroaching forest. Bethany stood in front of the door, gazing at the scene. The lot was private and simply landscaped. Marcine's one flower garden, now covered in snow, displayed her love of birds with the number of houses and feeders taking up the space. A tarp covered what

Bethany imagined was a birdbath secured with rope to protect it from the brutal winter elements.

Bethany smiled. "My gran loves birds too. She caters to them more than she takes care of herself." She turned to Jana. "Sorry about your grandmother."

Jana stood in the archway between the dining and living rooms. "Thank you. She was a great person. Quite the artist too." Jana pointed to the hutch on the sideboard. "Bird-watching wasn't just a hobby for her. Those are all of hers."

Bethany crossed the room to the hutch. Palm-sized bird sculptures sat on the shelves of the hutch, each one more intricate than the next. "She made these?"

Nate moved away from the table to stand next to her. "Yes, and who knows how many more."

Bethany marveled at the details—the multilayered wings with striated feathers, the beaded eyes, the varied shapes of the beaks. Some were painted in fantastical colors, though Bethany could still identify the birds because of Marcine's eye for detail. Her favorite by far was the pine grosbeak with its heavy chest and hawkish beak. Its breast was painted a rich garnet. The color accented beautifully the smoke feathers and the white-and-black details of his face and wing tips.

Bethany picked up the grosbeak. "They're stunning."

"She was always giving them away, never selling them, though she could have probably become well known for them. And she always made a male and female. Who knows how many pieces of hers are out there?"

"I love that she made pairs."

"I do too. But we don't have any matching pairs except for the orioles."

"That's too bad."

Nate's eyes bore into hers. "When I was little she used to tell me what each bird symbolized. I still remember them all."

"Really? What does the grosbeak symbolize?"

"Boldness and primal satisfaction." His gaze was steady. "Its call is said to awaken a quest from slumber."

She swallowed hard and quickly replaced the bird before she dropped it.

"Ask me another," he said, moving a step closer. He towered over her and could rest his chin on the top of her head if he wanted to.

She pointed to a delicate tawny bird with black spots and a beak as sharp as a pin.

He took it off the shelf. "Behold, the male flicker."

Bethany let him set the sculpture into her upturned palm.

"I love his coloring." She turned it over to study the signature. "Did she go by the name 'Mar'?"

"No, that's 'M.A.R.' for Marcine Arabeth Ransom," he said, his voice slightly hoarse.

Bethany studied the bird in her hand. "It's beautiful."

She looked up at Nate when the silence grew heavy and caught him staring at her. Their eyes locked for a few long seconds. The intensity of the moment made the heat rise to her face, and she could tell by how still he stood, and by the rise and fall of his chest, that their closeness affected him too. For that reason, she looked again at the ceramic piece and tried to control the slight tremor of her hand.

"Yes." He paused and stepped forward. "It is very beautiful." He was so close his breath warmed her cheek.

She turned to look for Jana, but the younger woman had disappeared.

Bethany set the bird back on the shelf and took a step away from the hutch. "So what's the symbolism behind the flicker?" She brushed her hands together.

Nate shoved his hands in his pockets. "Authenticity. Inspired energy." He cocked his head. "Spiritual healing of emotional wounds."

Her jaw tightened while the silence of the room pressed against Bethany from all sides.

"Speaking of which." She'd mumbled it so Nate leaned forward and turned an ear toward her.

"Excuse me?"

"What I came here for. I was sidetracked with meeting your sister and seeing the birds and such." She gripped the back of a chair. "Maybe we should sit down."

He pushed her chair in. "Wait. I know what you're going to say."

Bethany scowled. "You do?"

"Yes, I do. I'm not clueless. I can read people pretty well." He waved his hand dismissively. "A prerequisite of being a writer," he joked.

She crossed her arms. "Okay. Tell me then."

"You're going to tell me you don't want to see me anymore."

Bethany opened her mouth to say something—she didn't

know what—because her natural response was always to contradict. But he was right, of course. How could she respond with anything but the truth? Yet the longer he looked at her with that pleading, chocolate-eyed expression, the more she questioned herself.

"You don't have to say if I'm right or not. But I want to make a deal with you if that's okay." He squared his shoulders.

"A deal?"

"Yes. So the deal is that you go out with me one more time. If you still feel the same way about me afterward, then I won't bother you anymore."

Bethany sighed. "Nate?"

Those eyes begged for a chance. "Yes?"

"Why do you think I don't want to see you anymore?"

Nate pressed his lips together. "Because," he started, then shook his head. "Truthfully, I have no idea. But it seems like you've had a good time the last few times we've been together. If I didn't sense that, I wouldn't bother."

A few seconds passed between them while he looked away. He turned back to her. "I have to run to Duluth later in the week to finalize some paperwork with the house. Come with me. I'll take you to the best seafood restaurant in the upper Midwest. We can catch a movie. And I'll show you my license plate collection."

Bethany crossed her arms and laughed. "Oooh, tempting."

"Not many people are privy to so intimate a detail about me."

She shook her head, looking at her feet, chuckling. "You drive a hard bargain."

He bent slightly to see her face. "So it's a deal?"

Bethany nodded. "Yes, it is."

JANA REAPPEARED A SHORT TIME LATER AND ASKED Bethany if she would stay for dinner.

"Besides, it's Nate's turn in the kitchen tonight," she said with a wink.

"Maybe I should ask what kind of cook he is before I accept." Bethany looked sideways at him.

Nate snorted. "I take offense at that. No one has ever questioned my culinary skills."

Jana agreed. "He makes a wicked pasta alla Norma. You have to try it."

"I don't see how I can't stay now." Bethany clapped Nate on the shoulder. "You're reputation has been properly inflated. I hope you can live up to it."

"I hope so too," Nate said under his breath.

Jana pulled out a bucket and pine cleaner from beneath the sink. "I'm almost finished cleaning the guest room. Call me when dinner is ready," she said before leaving the room.

So Nate donned a calico apron and juggled the chilis and the garlic bulb until he offered to teach Bethany how to juggle.

"No, thanks. I'd rather watch you."

"As much as I'd like to spend the night impressing you, I think I'd better get to dicing." He pointed to the eggplant on the other end of the counter. "I'll need that, please."

Bethany handed it to him. "You cook, juggle, write, do yoga—"

He lifted an eyebrow. "I wouldn't count yoga in my skill set."

"You're a regular Renaissance man." Bethany pulled out a chair and sat down.

"You have no idea," he said, his eyes back on the cutting board. "I'm a one-man wonder."

Sitting at the dining room table afforded her the view of him bent over the counter, cutting eggplant with the precision of a surgeon. Bethany silently appraised Nate for the next twenty minutes while they talked, lingering on his long, lean form since his attention was focused elsewhere for once. She loved how unpretentious and self-deprecating he was, and he made her laugh too. Bethany took a drink from her water glass, rolling an ice cube into her mouth, then set the glass down to put her head in her hands. There she went again, focusing on how wonderful he was when she came there earlier to break contact with him.

"Headache?"

Bethany startled. "Huh?" She crunched down on the ice cube.

"You're holding your head like it hurts."

Bethany straightened. "It does. No, it doesn't. Not like that. I—"

He opened one of the cabinets above his head. "There's some ibuprofen somewhere here."

She got up to take it from him, but when he found it in the cabinet, it slipped from his fingers. As he tried catching it, the bottle somersaulted through the air, landing with a wet-sounding *plop* into the boiling marinara sauce. Without thinking, he tried fishing it out with his bare hand.

Bethany managed to make a warning sound but it was too late. The agony on Nate's face was instant. He jerked his hand out of the pot, splattering sauce droplets everywhere as he tried to shake away the pain.

"Oh, Nate!"

Bethany grabbed his wrist in one hand, and opened the refrigerator door with the other. "Butter! Where's the butter?" She fumbled around in the door, pulled opened some drawers, bent down to look on the bottom shelf. No butter.

"Don't have any," he said through gritted teeth. Already the skin on his thumb looked shiny as a blister formed underneath the surface.

She groaned. Before realizing what she was doing, Bethany pulled his hand forward and stuck his thumb in her mouth.

They looked at each other for a few frozen moments.

Nate was wide-eyed. "What...are you doing?"

Bethany yanked his thumb out of her mouth and dabbed at it with a paper towel.

"I, uh...the ice...in my mouth...I thought it'd be the quickest relief." She couldn't look him in the eye. What was she thinking? "Sorry. That was a little—"

Nate exhaled. "Yeah, a little...something, but I tell you what: I'm going to burn my hand more often if that's your idea of a remedy."

Bethany glanced away because the light in Nate's eyes was an inferno. Still gripping his wrist, she led him over to the faucet and ran the cold water over his poor thumb. She refused to look at him.

She cleared her throat. "Honey will work too if you have some. Or vanilla."

"Sounds good," he whispered.

In an overhead cabinet, Bethany spotted a bottle of vanilla. She soaked a corner of the paper towel with the brown liquid and pressed it into his thumb.

"How soon will dinner be ready?" Jana squeezed her face between them. "Smells heavenly."

"Twenty minutes or so. Nate burned himself with the sauce." Bethany tossed the towel in the garbage. "He'll need a bandage." Thank goodness for Jana. Something needed to put out the fire in Nate's eyes.

Jana winced when she looked at his thumb. "Cooking comes with certain risks." She looked at Bethany. Under her breath, she said, "My guess is he's distracted. He's usually not so clumsy."

Nate huffed. "I'm right here, you know. You could be a little more discreet with your insults," he said, stifling a smile.

Despite his injured hand, Nate pulled off his pasta alla Norma dish with serious aplomb. The three of them opened the bottle of wine that Jana ran to D & G to buy last minute and clinked glasses. Bethany watched Jana as the younger woman teased her brother relentlessly about everything: his clumsiness in the kitchen, the uneven line of stubble along his jawline, even how he held his wineglass with a pinkie hooked in midair. He took it good-naturedly and dished it back. Bethany liked being in the midst of their camaraderie, something she'd missed as an only child.

By the time they finished the wine and cleared the dishes from the table, it was late. Really late. Jana thanked Bethany for staying, for giving her and Nate a break from the tedium of sorting through their grandmother's things. Then Nate held out Bethany's coat to her.

"I'll walk you out," he said.

A heavy blanket of stars hung overhead as they followed the curved brick walk to the driveway. The sound of their footsteps crunching on the ice-packed snow seemed to echo more loudly in the stillness. A dusting of snow covered Bethany's car, and she watched while Nate cleared off the windshield with his coat sleeve. Bethany breathed deeply to clear her lungs.

When she reached for her door handle, Nate's hand covered hers, a gentle yet urgent touch.

"I'm glad you stayed," he said softly. "That you didn't... do what you meant to do."

His hand was so warm on hers.

She struggled with a response, the words sitting on her tongue like little weights. "I had a really nice time." Despite that voice inside her head that repeated *Stop, Bethany* over and over, she took a step toward him.

Nate's eyes drifted over her face and settled on her lips. "I did too."

Bethany sensed him drawing closer, little by little. She stiffened, waiting for the initial touch, and clenched her free hand at her side. It was taking so achingly long, this first kiss, and when she looked at him, she wondered if he was afraid, afraid she'd stop him. But then he slowly dipped his head and brushed his mouth against hers in a slow, leisurely way. He tasted of peppermint.

Bethany heard the hush of traffic passing by on Highway 61 and her own breathing, light yet uneven. She heard the sigh of branches brushing against each other, and an engine rev nearby. She also heard his slight intake of breath. She held her breath, afraid any unnecessary sound or movement would break the spell, and then she wouldn't be able to help herself. She'd pull away once she realized what she was getting herself into.

But on the contrary, once their lips touched, Bethany stepped closer, wrapping her arms around his back, balancing on tiptoe to fit more snugly against his chest and into his embrace. The kiss was more than she could hope for in a first kiss: unhurried, full of passion, and a hint of danger. Danger in that she knew there wouldn't be just this one kiss. Not by a long shot.

After a while, he drew back.

Bethany licked her bottom lip. "I should go." She gripped the door handle tighter.

A dog howled nearby, a low, mournful sound. It was followed by another dog's bark, closer still, which startled both of them. Bethany turned in the direction of the sound and his hand fell away from her arm.

Nate stuffed his hands in his pockets and rocked back on his heels. He chuckled under his breath.

Bethany opened her door but paused before getting in. "What's so funny?"

The shadows made his dark eyes blaze like hot coals. "So many obstacles for such a simple course."

"What's that supposed to mean?"

He kicked at a chunk of compacted snow stuck near the wheel well of the car. "It means I'll see you later this week." He looked down at her. "Good night," he said simply.

"Good night," she said, but he'd already turned back to the house.

Bethany got into her car and watched him retrace his steps along the sidewalk. She touched the spot on her lips where the feeling of his kiss still lingered. Yet, despite the lightheaded sensation that made her rest her head against the back of her seat, a small seed of sadness planted itself in her throat. She tried swallowing it as she backed out of the driveway and onto Water Street, but the feeling didn't go away. What had she expected to happen between them once she allowed their relationship to get this far? Of course she'd fall hard for him; he was perfect for her. But that would make it that much harder to break it off when the time came. She'd made it no secret that she wasn't looking for a commitment, especially because of his limited time in Hendricks.

Despite the rules she'd imposed on her relationship with Nate Ransom, Bethany might end up the loser in her own game.

Chapter Ten

A few mornings later, Nate met with Del Arbuckle, a lifelong local who ran an auction service when he wasn't tending an organic farm on his property near Sheevy's Lake. Del liked to talk, and his topics mostly centered around town gossip, which might have been entertaining if Nate could associate the names with faces. The man kept a small office on Mill Street under the same roof as an insurance agency and a massage therapist, with dark paneled walls and a framed movie poster of *Smokey and the Bandit* hanging above his desk. Ironing out the details of the estate auction and the eventual sale of the house took fifteen minutes. Del dominated the rest of the hour-long meeting with a passionate discussion about his beloved Minnesota Wild, the most talented hockey team in the league despite what the standings showed. Nate left Del's office with the older man's voice vibrating in his head like a buzz saw and in need of fresh air.

He walked along Mill, fighting against the bitter wind blowing in from the lake a block away. It darted between the buildings and through the streets, snapping the flag outside the post office, forcing the few people who came out for errands to scurry into and out of shops or their vehicles like colorfully bundled beetles. Despite the frigid temperate, Nate walked in the opposite direction of his car, not certain where he was headed until he found himself looking toward the back entrance of Manipura Yoga as he crossed High Street. Bethany's car was parked in its usual spot.

He kept walking. As much as he wanted to see her, Nate sensed she struggled with some inner demons lately. She'd hinted at it during the night in the ice shelter before their abrupt departure. She'd mentioned the distant relationship with her parents. Bethany was attracted to Nate, that was clear, but she'd found reasons to keep him at arm's length so far. So he'd give her space.

Crossing the street, Nate ducked into Two Tree Coffee before his scheduled phone interview for a writing assignment. The place hummed with activity, coffee-fueled chatter competing with the music playing over the speakers. The atmosphere was an eclectic mix of upholstered armchairs, repurposed pallets turned into tables, and local art. Overhead in the center of the room, a vintage rowboat hung from the ceiling by cables, strands of ivy trailing overboard. It was a fun, cozy vibe.

In line, he ordered, paid, and gave his name to the cashier.

"You're Nate Ransom? The writer?"

Nate turned around to seek out the self-assured voice

and found an attractive woman with a dark curtain of hair swept over one shoulder standing behind him in line. She looked at him purposefully and raised her already arched eyebrows into the stratosphere when he took a few extra seconds to respond.

He shifted on his feet. "All my life. And you are?"

Her hand shot out and gripped his with surprising force. "I'm Paige Goff. I've read your work in the *Duluth Herald*. Actually, it was your piece in *Travel America* about Chicago's architectural tours that first caught my eye."

Flattered, he stepped out of line with his coffee and stood next to her while she ordered.

"I'm not used to being singled out for my work, especially outside of Duluth."

She handed a bill to the cashier for her drink. "I'm a photographer, so noticing bylines is part of my job."

"Are you on staff somewhere? Freelance?"

Paige held her coffee to the side while she stuffed change into her small backpack then slung it over her shoulder. "A little bit of both. Wanna sit down?"

Nate checked his phone. "I only have a few minutes before an appointment."

"My coat is at that table over there," she said, pointing it out to him.

Coffee in hand, Nate waited near the table while she added cream and sugar to her cup at the side counter, feeling partly obligated to chat since she'd recognized his name. But he also didn't care for her presumptuousness, how making his appointment on time seemed secondary to their conversation.

Paige set her bag at her feet and sat down with some effort, a small grimace passing over her face like a shadow. "Old injury," she explained, motioning to the chair opposite her. "Can you stay?"

Nate sat, controlling the deep breath he took so he wouldn't exhale in frustration.

She studied him with an overly done smile. "In answer to your question, I'm a regular contributor to a couple magazines, but I mostly do freelance. You might have seen my work." She stirred her coffee.

He took the bait. "What have you done?"

"You know that photo of the L.A. cop whose canine partner got shot in a drug bust gone wrong? The one where he's sitting in the parking lot with the dog? I took that."

Nate pictured the photo immediately. It first appeared on social media last summer, and it had already been shared thousands of times by the time he saw it. It tugged at his heartstrings, the expression of the cop as he held the dog's head in his lap while the German shepherd looked directly into the camera. It was powerful, upsetting, and achingly beautiful.

"No kidding. That went viral pretty quick." He didn't miss the feigned modesty in how she lifted her shoulder.

"Pure serendipity."

Nate winced. He wouldn't exactly call photographing a dog injured in the line of duty "serendipity." It sounded insensitive. Opportunistic.

"So what brings you to Hendricks?"

Paige raked her fingers through the ends of her hair. "I'm actually here for a feature on the North Shore. I've been talking with the Stetmans at Sturgeon Widows Tours."

Nate took a sip of his coffee and nodded. "Great company."

"I actually used to date Sean Stetman."

He wasn't sure why she needed to tell him that and didn't know how to respond. Nate looked again at his phone.

"Are you local?" she asked hurriedly.

"Used to be. I moved away when I was a kid, but my grandparents lived here."

She leaned back. "Ah. So you're visiting."

"Actually, I'm here to settle my grandmother's estate."

"Oh. Sorry."

He nodded. "So what magazines have you worked with?"

"Have you heard of *Outdoors* and *On the Edge*? Those are two that I appear in most regularly."

"Of course. I've actually submitted a few things to—"

"Yeah, I just had a photo spread in *Edge* in November. Top five secret climbing destinations in Argentina or something like that," she said, shrugging it off like having work appear in one of the most prestigious outdoor magazines was as easy as submitting a wedding announcement to the local paper.

Nate had had enough. He got up and pushed in his chair. "I've really got to run. It was nice meeting you."

Paige pulled a business card out of her wallet. "Maybe we can work together sometime."

He didn't miss the way she cocked her head when she handed him the card. He'd seen that sort of look from

women before. It tended to mean they'd be seeing him
again if they had any say in the matter.

"Maybe. Nice to meet you," he said, stuffing the card in
his back pocket. He had no intention of working with Paige
Goff or keeping her card, for that matter.

And he left the coffee shop wishing Bethany would give
him that look sometime soon.

TWO HOURS LATER, NATE FINISHED TRANSCRIBING
his handwritten notes from the interview into a document
on his laptop when Bethany's name flashed across his
phone as a text. He pushed his laptop aside on the dining
table so he could give his full attention to her.

Are you still willing to put up with me on your trip to Duluth?

Flushed with the thrill, Nate grinned and texted back:

Only if you promise not to mess with my mojo

What 'mojo' you have can be credited to you having a cool sister.

I can't argue with that.

They volleyed flirty insults back and forth for a few
minutes that left Nate almost breathless. Whatever barriers
she set up when they got together seemed to disappear
when they texted or talked on the phone. Bethany was as
bold and witty as he hoped she'd be before he walked into
her studio two weeks ago.

Nate typed another response but before he could send it,
his phone rang.

"Texting is so inefficient." Her voice was throaty,
sensual.

Nate smiled. "Again, you are so right."

"I was just thinking about you," she said.

His heart quickened. "Tell me more."

"I was looking out my window just now and saw a flicker on Gran's feeder."

"They're stunning, aren't they?" He looked up to where the flicker figurine rested on the shelf in front of him.

"Very. It reminded me of your grandmother's sculpture. What was its meaning again?"

"Authenticity. Energy. Healing of emotional wounds."

"Interesting." A few seconds passed. Bethany cleared her throat. "Anyway, what time should I be ready tomorrow?"

They settled on a time. She had a full day of classes but would be packed and ready to go by five o'clock. After they'd said goodbye, he looked at the weather forecast and groaned. Snow and more snow, starting tomorrow morning.

Nate shut his laptop and ran his fingers through his hair. There was no way he'd let a little snow ruin his plans. Worst-case scenario was they'd have to take it slow, maybe miss dinner out in Duluth and stay a little later on Saturday before the roads were cleared.

The next forty-eight hours were important. If Bethany didn't give him a solid sign that she wanted their relationship to continue, he'd back off. Nate was totally invested while she kept backpedaling. He didn't want her to spend time with him because she had trouble telling him no. But he also couldn't imagine being in Hendricks, or anywhere for that matter, without having Bethany in his life now that they had reconnected. He had to make this work between them. He just had to.

Chapter Eleven

If Bethany had listened to Gran earlier, she could be curled under a fleece throw on her futon watching movies. Instead, she squinted through the Rover's windshield at the heavy curtain of snow coming down in the otherwise inky night. Gran warned her about the forecast, but Bethany decided against cancelling the trip to Duluth with Nate. She and Nate had just passed the "You are Now Leaving Twin Rivers" sign. That meant they were twenty miles from Hendricks. So far they'd been driving an hour.

Bethany cleared her throat. "At this rate we'll be in Duluth by midnight." She instantly regretted her words. Next to her, Nate gripped the steering wheel with both hands. He'd been pretty quiet since they left town as he concentrated on the road.

"I'm thinking we should pull off once we get to Sterling. If I remember right, there's a motel—"

Suddenly a mighty *whump!* shook the car.

"Oh!" Bethany's hand shot out to the dashboard.

"Great. Hold on," Nate said as he turned the wheel into the slide.

The disjointed feeling of spinning out of control twisted Bethany's stomach as the Rover made a wide, sweeping circle in reverse. The car hit a bank of snow and slid sideways at an angle for a few harried seconds. She'd never gone off the road before, but Bethany knew they were on their way to being good and stuck.

The Rover stopped abruptly. Its front end pointed nose down toward the shallow ditch. Ahead, an imposing wall of snow-draped bushes stared them down.

She and Nate looked at each other for a few frozen seconds in the glow of the dashboard lights. Then Nate let his head drop against the back of the seat.

"News flash: we won't be going to Duluth tonight," he said while looking at the ceiling.

"On the bright side, if my sense of direction isn't back there on the road, I'd say we're pretty lucky." Bethany twisted in her seat to look behind them, but seeing anything through the rear window was impossible. "Since we just passed through Twin Rivers, there's that stretch with the really steep drop-off on the right near the river just outside of town."

Nate tapped the wheel forcibly with the heel of his hand. "Still."

Bethany unbuckled herself. "What happened?"

"I think we blew a tire. And the Rover didn't like that snowy patch with only three tires is my guess."

Fat flakes floated in front of the headlights. The forecast

called for two to four overnight. Bethany guessed four inches had already fallen, and it wasn't letting up any time soon.

"Sit tight," Nate said. "I'm going to see if I can see how deep we're stuck. Not that it'll do any good." He found a flashlight in the center console. "Maybe I can get a look at the tires."

Nate pushed on the door. It wouldn't budge. He leaned into it with his shoulder, inching it open a little, but it held fast against whatever prevented it from opening on the other side. "Can you get yours open?"

Bethany tried her door, throwing her shoulder into it, expecting the same resistance, but it swung open easily and she almost fell out into the snow. She got out of the car and turned back to face Nate, who twisted out of his coat to give himself more room to maneuver.

"I don't think I can get my legs over there," he said.

He grunted and strained, pushing his seat back as far as it could go, and struggled to lift his right leg over the shift lever and into Bethany's seat area.

"I can't do it. Too tall," he said, contorted into an awkward mass of limbs. He unwound himself, falling back into his seat.

Laughing, Bethany braced herself against the door frame. Seeing Nate trying to fit his six-foot-six frame into the span of three feet was both funny and painful to watch. The laughter was cathartic. The more Nate squirmed, the harder it spilled out.

Nate stopped struggling to watch her, a winsome smile

on his face. "I'm glad that my sorry self is a source of amusement for you," he said, chuckling.

Bethany wiped melted snow from her cheeks with the back of her mittened hands. "I'm sorry. It's just that—" she looked behind her toward the highway—"I think it's partly because of you and part delirium." She turned toward him. "I think we'll be camping here tonight."

"That would be correct."

Again, Nate tried twisting himself out of the seat. This time he succeeded in sliding backward through the space above the middle console and into the backseat. His legs resting on the console, he wore a self-congratulatory smirk. Bethany laughed even harder.

"Now what?" She wiped the tears from the corners of her eyes.

"Now I get out."

The back door opened easily when Nate tried it. Outside, he used his folding shovel to dig around the tires while Bethany held a flashlight. The flat tire revealed itself when they worked over the second tire.

"I'd better call Jana and let her know we're out here. Someone needs to know," he said, refolding the shovel. "Should you tell your grandmother?"

Telling Gran would only upset her. For all Gran knew, Bethany was on her way to Duluth and would arrive safely in a few hours. Gran didn't need to know how their plan literally veered off the road.

The car had carved a wide path through the snow on its slide down the short embankment. The snowplows would be up and down the highway all night long, blowing mounds onto the sides of the road. She pulled her hood over her head.

"We should probably call the police too. We'll be buried if the plows don't know we're here. Maybe they'll give us a ride to town."

Nate groaned. "No one in their right mind would come out here tonight." He rubbed his hands together.

Bethany rubbed her arms. "Can we continue this conversation *inside* the car?"

"Good idea."

He opened the back door and flipped the seat down. From a blue tote, he pulled out two sleeping bags and a pile of blankets. When he'd arranged everything, Nate stepped aside and let her crawl into the back.

Bethany smoothed the bumps out of the wool blankets and moved over, waiting for Nate. She patted the space beside her. "Coming in?"

Even in the dark with heavy snow coming down, Nate's discomfort showed in the downward slant of his brows, the firm set to his mouth. Bethany didn't know what to make of it. He'd been pursuing her for almost three weeks now, yet he seemed reluctant to be near her. After several seconds, he pulled himself into the Rover, reaching behind him to shut the door. Nate fumbled in the dark for the small battery-powered lantern and switched it on, blinding them with the sudden glare.

"On second thought," Nate said, turning it off. "Maybe we should save the battery."

"Good idea."

By the time Nate unrolled the sleeping bags from their

cases and spread them lengthwise, Bethany's eyes adjusted to the darkness again. The snow cast a heavenly calm inside the vehicle. The front windshield was already covered with a layer of snow. Nate settled with his back against the side window, blew into his hands, then folded them into his lap. His eyes blazed into hers across the short space.

Bethany couldn't keep the smile off her face.

"What's so funny?"

She pressed the back of her hand into her mouth and looked away from him, trying to compose herself. After a while, she coughed. "It's just an interesting way to spend a Friday night is all."

That wasn't really what made her laugh, but she couldn't tell him how obvious his discomfort looked to her or that she tucked her hands underneath her legs to keep her body from shaking. Having been at constant war with herself the last few weeks about her feelings for Nate, Bethany worried. Her attraction to him was undeniable. Should she get involved with him when there were no guarantees? Until she made up her mind, Bethany needed a cool head, though the rest of her body wasn't cooperating.

He hooked his hands behind his neck. "You mean this isn't ideal to you? Sliding into a ditch has always worked with my other dates."

"It depends on what else the date involves. If we sit here and stare at each other all night until we fall asleep, it wouldn't be quite as interesting as—" Bethany's voice trailed off when she couldn't come up with something that fit the bill.

"As what?" A lazy smile spread across his face.

Panicked, she blurted the first thing that came to mind. "As playing a game."

His shoulders dropped slightly. "A *game?*"

"Sure."

"What do you have in mind?"

Bethany rested her chin on her chest, thinking. Then she snapped her fingers. "Got it. I'll ask you a question with two possible answers. You choose the one you'd prefer."

"Is this that Would You Rather game?"

"You don't like that one?" Maybe suggesting a game was a mistake. The awkwardness of their situation was increasing by the second.

He shrugged.

Bethany turned to look out the window. It was going to be a long night with Nate brooding in the dark, cold car. His mood was starting to wear off on her.

He nudged her thigh with his foot. "On second thought, ask me one. You surprised me is all."

"Just trying to pass the time." She straightened. "So here goes. Would you rather be in here with me for twenty-four hours or on a dinner date in a restaurant for two hours?"

"Maybe you should save that question for tomorrow morning. We've only been locked up together for what, ten minutes?"

Bethany chuckled. "Good point. How about this one: would you rather find your true love or a suitcase with five million dollars inside?"

"What if my true love was a multimillion-dollar heiress? What if the money in the suitcase allowed me to buy a penthouse in a Manhattan skyscraper where I met my true love?"

She laughed. "This isn't how the game is played." Bethany rummaged around in her bag. "While you think about your answer, I'm going to look in here for something to eat. I'll be too hungry to fall asleep tonight."

Nate tipped the blue tub toward him, searching for something. He tossed her a box.

"Would you rather eat Bubba Bars or go to bed hungry?"

She held the box up so she could see the label in the dim light. "Bubba Bars? The last time I had these I was too young to read the box."

"No one can say I'm not prepared."

"Gran used to buy these for me by the caseload." Bethany opened the box and tore the wrapper off one. The chocolate-frosted granola bar wasn't the salmon croquette dinner Nate had promised her, but it would have to do. She offered him one. They ate in silence for several minutes until Nate leaned over on his side. He stretched his legs and rolled over onto his back.

"Do your parents ever come to Hendricks to see you and your grandmother?"

Why was he bringing this up again? Bethany took another bite of her bar while she thought about how she should respond.

"Would you rather not talk about your parents ever again or listen to me recite the periodic table?" he asked.

"Very funny," she said. "Do you think if you turn it into a game I'll be more willing to talk?"

"I don't want you to talk about anything that makes you uncomfortable."

Bethany crumpled her wrapper, tucked it in her coat pocket, then stretched out alongside Nate. She could see the whites of his eyes in the dim light when she turned to look at his profile. "Would you rather live the next fifty years in Hendricks or spend the rest of your life traveling the world, never staying in the same place for more than three days?"

Nate blew air out of his cheeks. "I like to travel but not that much. Definitely Hendricks."

"Do you like living in Duluth?"

He hesitated. "It's nice enough. My mom and dad are there." He turned his head toward her. "Do you wish you lived somewhere else?"

She'd liked Marquette well enough; the two colleges in close proximity gave it a bustling young vibe. But when she graduated with her degree and grew restless in her job, Hendricks drew her back.

"Not really. Hendricks is home for now."

Nate hooked his hands behind his head. "I have another question for you," he said, sliding a little closer until he was shoulder to shoulder with her. Bethany turned toward him. The snowy landscape outside highlighted half his face; the other half was shrouded in darkness. Still she could see he was grinning.

"Go ahead."

"Would you rather kiss me for a full minute now or for twenty minutes in the morning?"

Her eyes widened as she stared at him. Then she tapped

her finger against her chin in mock consideration. "There's the morning breath thing to consider."

His grin broadened as he turned on his side, propping himself up on one elbow.

Bethany looked at him. "But a full minute isn't nearly time enough—"

Nate kissed her.

A jolt pulsed through Bethany like a lightning bolt, and she involuntarily stiffened at the surprise. When his hand cupped her chin, however, so that their lips met in perfect alignment, she melted against him. Bethany had no idea how long the kiss lasted, but when her hand started tingling from being pinned against her hip, she pulled away and shifted.

"You broke the rules. That was over a minute," she breathed against his cheek. "You lose."

"I'll gladly accept defeat." His voice was barely a whisper as he kissed her again. He touched her face, running his fingers along her jaw, tilting her chin so that their lips touched ever so slightly. "What will happen tomorrow when we get out of this ditch? When we're back in Hendricks?"

Bethany breathed against his mouth because she couldn't hold her breath any longer.

"The more important question is what will happen when you go back to Duluth?"

Nate kissed the corner of her mouth, nibbled on her bottom lip. He pulled away, looking at her.

"What do you want to happen?" he asked.

Bethany hesitated. It wasn't that she didn't know what to hope for between her and Nate. At the moment, she was as sure as she'd ever been about anything. Nate Ransom was perfect as far as she could tell, and she'd like to spend time—a long time—getting to know him better. Bethany just didn't know how she could ask Nate to stay in Hendricks, to not leave after his grandmother's house sold. That was the problem. She had no right to ask that of him. And then his inevitable answer would open an old wound. He couldn't stay. His life was in Duluth. What then?

But when Nate's hand slipped behind her head in the next moment and he lowered her down against the blankets, his lips traveling from her mouth, along her jawline, to her neck, Bethany closed her eyes and pushed those worries aside for the rest of the night.

BETHANY BLINKED AGAINST THE HARSH MORNING light when she opened her eyes. Cocooned in the sleeping bag with Nate's face pressed against the back of her head, Bethany could barely move. She luxuriated in the feeling of his arm wrapped around her waist, and she ran her hand along his arm, pulling it tighter against her. She didn't want to move. It was so warm underneath the layers. The small portion of her face exposed to the chill inside the Rover convinced her to stay still lest she wake Nate and lose his body heat.

But something had awakened her, something vibrating near her hip.

Her phone.

She dug underneath her and touched the hard rectangle,

but it was outside of the sleeping bag. Reluctantly, she sat up and searched for it. Her breath clouded inside the Rover.

Gran's number was on the screen. She tapped to connect.

"Gran?"

"You're still in Duluth, aren't you?"

A white-hot dart of worry shot through Bethany's chest. Gran's voice was off. "What's wrong?" She glanced at Nate, who threw off the blankets and sat up, his forehead wrinkling.

"I-I'm not feeling my usual self."

"What do you mean?"

"Oh, it's probably nothing. I'm sure it's all the baking and cleaning I did yesterday for the book club meeting. My arm feels numb, and I just—I just am really lightheaded. Not thinking straight."

"Oh Gran. No, I'm not back yet. But you need to get to the hospital."

"No, I don't. I probably didn't get enough sleep. I'll just lie back down until you get home."

"No, this sounds a little more serious than being tired."

"Really, I'll be fine until you get home."

Nate kicked the rest of the covers off and pulled on his coat. Within a minute, he opened the door. Outside, he held his phone to his ear.

Bethany tried slipping her own coat on one-handed. "Listen to me. I'm going to hang up and call Darcy. She's going to take you to the hospital. You need to get checked out, okay?"

Gran sighed. "Fine. But I'm telling you it's just the effects of a busy day. You'll see."

"Well, thanks for indulging me. I'll be home as soon as I can. Love you."

When Gran hung up, Bethany slipped her other arm into her coat, pulled on her boots, and gathered the rest of her things that mingled with Nate's—her scarf, gloves, and hat —and stuffed everything into her overnight bag.

Her heart pounded. She checked on Nate's whereabouts and found him circling the Rover, surveying their situation. His expression was grim.

Guilt gripped Bethany. Her fingers shook as she found Darcy's name in her contacts. She chided herself for being so carefree, for agreeing to the Duluth trip even when she knew about the travel advisory. If she didn't get out of this ditch in a hurry, if something happened to Gran, she'd never forgive herself for being so irresponsible.

Chapter Twelve

✦❧✦

Nate drifted up from a deep, uninterrupted sleep, which had been fueled by the flannel-and-down-wrapped nest he lay in and the warmth of Bethany next to him.

Only, Bethany wasn't there.

And when her voice came to him from far away, muffled, and growing in urgency as the seconds passed, he sat up to rub the sleep from his eyes.

Bethany held her phone to her ear. She shot him a worried look. After listening to the one-sided conversation with Gran for a minute, Nate pulled on his coat and laced up his boots. Checking for his own phone, he pushed open the door.

Another thigh-high drift had accumulated against the side of the Rover overnight. He waded through it to an area a short distance away where the snow wasn't so deep under the boughs of a fir. He'd call one of the two garages listed in Two Rivers for a tow, though he'd bet they'd been booked since the snow started falling last night. He paced along the tree line, casting glances toward the road every time a vehicle went by. The highway must be relatively clear; the cars moved past at a decent clip.

Nate connected with Two Rivers Auto and made arrangements for someone to come out for him and Bethany. He trudged through the snow, up to the road, for a mile marker and landmark, any small clue of where they might be. He stood on the shoulder, squinting in the blinding whiteness all around. A truck slowed down as it passed him. Nate waited, the phone still at his ear, as a man got out, yellow tow strap in hand.

"Need some help?" the man called.

Nate glanced toward the Rover. Even through the car's window, he could see Bethany's concern for Gran written on her face.

"You have no idea."

The Rover was back on the highway in twenty minutes after Nate hooked up the towline. Nate held on to Bethany as they made their way up to the highway through the powdered sugar snow. He eased the car back onto the highway, alternating between glancing at Bethany and watching the road. She sighed again, the third time in less than a minute.

"Gran isn't one to exaggerate. Numbness and balance issues are warning signs of—" Bethany glanced out her side window and paused. She shook her head slightly as if dismissing the thought. "Thank goodness Darcy was able to take her."

Nate reached over to take Bethany's hand where it rested in her lap. He held it for a few minutes until she picked up her phone to check for messages, reluctantly letting it go. Keeping his eyes on the road was secondary to watching the range of emotions cloud Bethany's face. Anger, worry, and frustration competed in equal measure. He hated himself for liking the feel of her hand in his while she fretted about her grandmother.

As they drove in silence, the sunlight sliced through the fir trees as they rounded the curve outside of Hendricks. Though it was still early, the snow-covered road had grown wet in spots as the salt worked its magic on the icy patches. A few minutes later, Nate pulled the Rover next to the ER entrance at Broman County Hospital. Bethany opened the door before he came to a complete stop.

"I'll be right in after I park," he said, but she'd already closed the door behind her.

A few minutes later, they followed a receptionist through the emergency room until he swept aside one of the fabric curtains and there was Bethany's grandmother, resting on a bed, eyes closed. They'd already hooked her up to an IV. Red digital numbers blinked on the monitor in the corner of the room with her vitals. Bethany sat down hard on one of the plastic chairs against the wall and took a deep breath. She reached for her grandmother's hand through the side rail.

Donna Marconi's eyes popped open. She noticed Nate first then realized Bethany sat beside her.

"I thought I'd died and gone to heaven for a second," she whispered from the side of her mouth to Bethany, though her words registered clearly with Nate. "Is this *him*?"

Bethany nodded, ducking her head to hide the smile.

"I can certainly see Marcine in him." Donna eyed him like she was judging the pie-eating contest at the county fair. Nate wouldn't be surprised if she licked her lips. He took a step back.

"Gran, he can hear you."

"I don't care," she whispered again.

Bethany's eyes grew wide in apology when she looked at Nate yet the smile lingered. "Nate, this is my grandmother, Donna Marconi."

Gran held her free hand out and Nate came forward to take it. "Sorry to meet you under such appalling circumstances," she said.

"Nice meeting you. And no worries. What's important is finding out what's wrong." He let go of her hand.

Bethany sat forward. "Has the doctor been here yet?"

Gran waved dismissively. "Of course. Long enough to tell me he didn't know anything just yet. And inform me there will be tests, of course. Lots of tests." She lifted her head, trying to see around the curtain.

Nate cleared his throat. "From what Bethany told me, it's for the best." He'd glanced at her vitals when the monitor beeped a minute ago. Blood pressure numbers shouldn't register that high.

Gran let out an exasperated groan and pressed the back of her head into the pillow. "I really believed I was invincible. By the way, Darcy and Sean went to find the cafeteria after the doctor left."

Bethany patted her grandmother's hand and glanced at Nate, the worry written plainly on her face. He leaned against the wall. Should he stay here to give Bethany support or leave and let them have privacy?

As if reading his mind, Bethany smiled and mouthed "thank you."

Gran's eyes were closed yet her brows dipped together. "On the bright side, I'm not dead yet."

Bethany snorted. "Leave it to you to make light of your hospital visit."

"You know me." She opened her eyes when the monitor beeped again.

"I'm just worried. I've been missing in action a lot lately," Bethany said. "I should be helping you more around the house." Bethany cast a quick glance in Nate's direction then clamped her hands into her lap.

Nate looked down at his feet. A guilty twinge tickled his gut. He'd taken up much of her time lately. He'd kept her away from her grandmother when Donna needed her most.

"Nonsense. If anything, you should be out more for someone your age instead of looking after your decrepit grandmother."

"Please, Gran. Don't try to blow this off as nothing."

"I'm also not going to blow it out of proportion," she said, fluffing the hair on the back of her head before settling into the pillow. "Your drama knows no bounds."

"Saying that you need help around the house is not being dramatic. It's realistic. You're not thirty years old anymore, even if you act closer in age to me than your friends most of the time."

"Age isn't important unless you're wine or cheese, dear."

Bethany crossed her arms. "You're lucky I love you, because I'm pretty annoyed by you right now."

At that point, Nate thought he should step out. He wondered if they minced their words with him in the room.

"I'm going to go grab a coffee or something."

Nate stuffed his hands in his pockets and pushed the curtain aside to get directions at the nurse's station. Behind him, the change in Bethany's hushed tone as she spoke to her grandmother when he left the room confirmed he'd made the right choice.

The cafeteria was in another annex, a short walk around the outside of the building. Nate breezed through the revolving doors, passed the darkened gift shop, and followed the scents of coffee and breakfast sausage.

It was a sunny room with walls covered in abstract paintings and a line of potted dragon trees in the far corner, their verdant spikes reaching toward the windows. Two workers wearing white hairnets and lime-colored T-shirts waited on the short line of people at the register.

Nate stepped up to the end of the line, glancing around the cafeteria while he waited his turn. A couple sat together at a table near the window, and the man did a double take when he saw Nate. Then the woman noticed her companion's reaction and followed his gaze too. Nate would bet the Rover they were Bethany's friends, Darcy and Sean.

Smiling, the woman left her seat and tentatively approached.

"Nate Ransom, right?"

Nate pulled his hands out of his pockets. "Yes, I am."

"I feel like I already know you with as much as Bethany talks about you." She stuck out her hand. "I'm Darcy Conti."

"I'm glad you were around to bring Donna in. It made the drive in a little less stressful for Bethany."

"Well, knowing Donna, she'll be out running errands this afternoon if she has anything to say about it." She tucked hair behind her ear and laughed. Darcy had an infectious smile, her eyes all but disappearing above an apple-cheeked grin. "So Bethany tells me you're a writer?"

"I am. I write for the Duluth newspaper and do a little freelancing on the side. Magazines mostly."

"We actually have had a photojournalist staying at the inn recently. Paige Goff, a photographer, is doing a feature on our tour company. You may have seen her work. She took the photo that went viral of the cop—"

"Yes. Holding the injured dog." Nate forced himself to keep the smile on his face. He'd encountered Paige Goff, in person and in conversation, one too many times.

"Right." Darcy cocked her head, studying him like she was seeing him through Bethany's eyes. She started when Sean came up behind her and introduced himself. Though average in height, Sean Stetman could be the poster boy for the Northwoods—rough-shaven, broad-shouldered, and chiseled in a way that suggested time spent outside overshadowed whatever indoor work he did.

The three of them chatted while Nate placed and waited

for his order. And then a few minutes later, coffee and breakfast sandwich in hand, Nate said goodbye.

"I guess we'll see you at the Red Hot Gala then," Darcy said as Sean slipped his arm around her like he had to do it often, pulling her away from conversations lest they go on forever.

"I'm looking forward to it." Nate balanced the sandwich on top of his coffee while he slipped the wallet into his back pocket. "Bethany's talked it up like it's the event of the century."

Darcy twisted away from Sean's arm. "If not this year, then for sure the next. I'm glad you'll still be in town."

Nate shrugged. "I'll actually be back in Duluth by then, but how could I pass up the invitation? It's worth the drive. *She's* worth the drive."

Her brows shot up. "Bethany tells me you've been spending a lot of time together."

Sean frowned at Darcy's statement. He whispered something in her ear, but she ignored him, turning her back to him.

"We have. She's a lot of fun."

She put her hands on her hip with a feigned warning. "Careful. Don't get any ideas about stealing her away from us."

Chuckling, Nate shook Sean's hand. "No immediate plans to," he said, which was a mistake. If Darcy was hungry for information about how serious he and Bethany had become, her expression turned positively ravenous at the "immediate" reference. There wasn't an ounce of doubt Darcy wished to see them together. In fact, her saccharine grin hinted Darcy would be reporting their conversation to Bethany as soon as possible.

Perfect.

He needed as much clout as possible so Bethany understood he wasn't just another boyfriend of the month, that he'd stick around if she let him.

Chapter Thirteen

✦❦✦

It was one of those mornings when Bethany wasn't anxious to start the day. Silda's steady purring as the cat rested on the pillow above her head almost lulled Bethany back to sleep, and the warmth underneath her comforter tempted her to cancel class. That idea was as fleeting as the sun poking its golden fingers through the blinds before she got out of bed. She had so much to do. The sun seemed to sense Bethany's mood, and it disappeared behind the clouds as soon as her feet touched the floor.

Part of her reluctance to get up was due to The Dream again. It had woken her a few times, causing a fitful night of hazy images and restless sleep. There were the usual elements—the cake, her family and friends, the rush to escape the burning house. But in this dream, instead of everyone making it safely outside, Gran and Nate chose to stay behind. Each time she reached for their hands to pull them outside, she grasped at air. As hard as she tried to entice them to follow her, Gran and Nate hung back in the dining room, an inferno raging around them. Finally the heat forced Bethany outside, where she collapsed in the grass, watching the flames eat away the house.

So she was tired. Fuzzy-headed, bone-weary exhausted. She didn't want to look in the mirror, sure as she was that every minute of lost sleep would be etched in the puffy skin under her eyes. As she sat on the edge of her bed, focusing on her breathing to wash the tension away, a cold draft raised goosebumps on her arms, like the front door was open. Bethany crossed the room and laid her hand on the radiator. Ice cold. The bathroom radiator was cold too.

If it weren't for Gran's health scare, a cold radiator wouldn't be the end of the world. But Gran was still in the hospital, and now her furnace was also in the midst of a medical emergency. Bethany gathered what she'd need to get ready for the day and headed down the sidewalk to Gran's empty but much warmer house.

After a quick breakfast and shower, and a call to a heating contractor, Bethany drove to the studio to get ready for her morning class before she picked up Gran. Bethany mulled over the doctor's assessment of Gran's condition while she crossed Highway 61. Dr. Kahlil had come into the room Saturday morning shortly after Nate left. While looking over Gran's chart, the doctor had used phrases like "transient ischemic attack" and "carotid endarterectomy," which Bethany asked her to put in layperson's terms. By the time Dr. Kahlil finished talking with her and Gran, Bethany's head spun. Gran had had a ministroke.

Bethany parked in her usual space along High Street and got out of her car, still stewing. While she gathered her bag and water bottle, Bethany wondered how she could help Gran. Well, she could insist Gran come in for yoga classes finally after years of prodding. She could also take control of the grocery shopping since Gran liked to shop with her sweet tooth. And Gran would have to curtail her card parties to once a week instead of two. Like it or not, Gran needed to drive in the slow lane from now on.

Shutting the door, Bethany decided to suffer the block-long walk to Two Tree Coffee for a mocha, a rare treat. She struggled to stay upright as she shuffled across the icy patches, wearing the bargain-bin flip-flops she'd bought at Grady's General Store before Christmas. Sometimes comfort trumped practicality, yet she wondered about her choice when she caught herself from slipping on a wide swath of ice in the alley.

Inside Two Tree, the warm ambience and scent of roasted beans soothed her somewhat as she scanned the eclectic coffee shop for familiar faces. With its mismatched tables, sofas, and well-worn upholstered chairs scattered on several levels, Two Tree Coffee owned the hipster vibe without trying too hard. Two former students from yoga class waved to Bethany when they noticed her standing in line, and she spent a few minutes chatting with one of her high school teachers, Lucy Dornbus, who happened to be moving back to town after spending the first five years of her retirement living in Ashland. Bethany missed the camaraderie of Hendricks for the three years she lived in Marquette. She'd made friends—she thankfully met Darcy there—but it wasn't a close-knit community like her hometown. Bethany knew most everyone in Hendricks.

Bethany said goodbye to Lucy, then scanned the menu board overhead for a minute even though she almost always ordered the same item. Carmen the barista, a tall girl with luminous eyes, waited while Bethany made up her mind.

"I'm feeling adventurous today. How about a toasted marshmallow mocha, please? And a cranberry-orange scone." Bethany pulled her wallet out of her bag.

"Gotcha." Carmen leaned forward like she didn't want anyone else to hear. "I keep meaning to tell you. Remember you introduced Ryan and me last spring during yoga class?"

Bethany chuckled while opening her wallet. "How could I forget? He'd only asked me to introduce you a thousand times since he was too shy to approach you on his own. Are you still dating?"

Carmen took a scone out of the case, beaming. "Yes. Nine months tomorrow."

"Congratulations! When's the wedding?"

The young girl's smile crinkled the skin around her eyes and she looked down as if embarrassed. "I wish I knew," Carmen whispered.

"Well, I expect an invite." Bethany dug in her wallet for money. "How much?"

Carmen looked at her sheepishly. "There's no charge."

"No charge?"

"Nope. He paid for you," she said, pointing to one of the far tables.

Bethany followed the direction Carmen pointed to where Nate sat with his back against the wall, one arm slung over the back of the chair next to him. Even from that distance, the effect of his eyes on her, sharply focused, boring into hers, made the blood rush to her head. She smiled despite the heaviness in her chest, and that was all he needed to get up and cross the space between them.

They hugged before either of them said anything. A light brush of his lips on hers was enough to send a charge through her body, and she tugged him closer by the coat lapel for a deeper kiss when he started to draw back. Bethany wanted that feeling to linger, to chase away the effects of last night and that morning, but they were surrounded by a coffeehouse full of people. Reluctantly, she let go.

"Hi there," he whispered when they drew apart. His eyes were hooded, full of desire.

She rubbed a shiny spot of her lip balm from the corner of his mouth. "The coffee trick was a nice surprise."

"You looked like you could use a lift," he said, searching her face.

"Thanks. I do."

"I was going to call, but since you're here I can tell you in person: I'm heading back to Duluth until Saturday. I've been away from work too long and need to catch up on a few things."

Nate's lips moved, but his voice seemed so far away. Bethany glanced over his shoulder at the other customers, distracted.

He shrugged. "Besides, Jana's back in school, and we basically have the house packed up and ready for the sale on Saturday. Del just has to send his guys over to take the boxes to the auction house." He cocked his head, still studying her. "Are you okay?"

Maybe it was the whirlwind weekend with Gran, her broken furnace, and now the news that Nate wouldn't be in Hendricks during the week. Whatever it was, a moistness crept into the corner of Bethany's left eye and she dabbed it with a finger. She didn't want to hear he was leaving. She didn't want to be alone when so many things seemed to be converging at once.

"Bethany?"

She shook her head, looking away to regain some composure. She wasn't a crier, and she certainly wasn't going to do it in public.

"Sorry." Her voice was husky with emotion. "I'm not usually like this." She waved a hand dismissively.

"Let's go to the table," he said. Nate took her mocha and touched Bethany's elbow, guiding her to the corner. After they sat down, Nate folded his hands on the tabletop. "What's going on?"

She massaged the muscles on the back of her neck. "I'm just overwhelmed is all. Gran has always been strong, healthy, willful Gran. Now I can just count on her being willful."

Nate's brows drew together. "So, she's coming home today, right?"

"Yes, I'm picking her up after class."

"I'll help you with anything. Anything. I mean it."

He brushed the top of her hand and intertwined his fingers with hers. His touch was so warm and soothing, a comfort. When Bethany looked up, he watched her intently.

She slipped her hand out from beneath his, tucking the hair behind her ear.

"Thanks. I appreciate that." She folded her hands into her lap to keep from fidgeting. "I just need to stay closer to home for a while now. I've been neglecting her."

"Whatever you want me to do—shovel, cook, take her to appointments during your classes—just tell me."

Bethany's gaze rested on his face. "But you just said you're going back to Duluth. How will you be able to help me if you're leaving?" It wasn't a question as much as it was an accusation. She regretted the tone of her voice, but not enough to apologize.

Nate looked away. "I could come back—"

"I'm thinking I'll have to cancel my classes for a while. But I'll keep that in mind." Bethany checked her phone. "Speaking of which, I really don't have time to stay. I have a class."

When Nate stood and slipped on his coat, the memories of Friday night flashed into Bethany's mind—the taste of his kiss, the way they kept each other warm underneath the woolen layers despite the frigid night. Her desire to be with him was overshadowed by the news that he wouldn't be back in town until the weekend. She hated that his absence, however short-term, bothered her.

"I won't keep you then," he said, his expression tight. "I'll call to check on you later."

Bethany turned to go but stopped when he reached for her hand.

"Goodbye," he said simply. His dark eyes, curtained by those black lashes, burned into hers. He leaned forward to kiss her lightly on the lips. "I'll see you on Friday?" he asked when they drew apart.

She looked down, nodding. "Yes, Friday. Thanks for the coffee."

Bethany met his eyes briefly. His worried expression ate at her, but she couldn't linger on it too long or she'd lose focus for the day ahead.

She wiggled her hand away from his. Without looking back, Bethany headed through the front door with her mocha in one hand, zipping her coat closed with the other. But despite the freezing temperatures, a warm sensation cocooned her in its folds as she retraced her steps through the alley. It wasn't on account of her coffee. He'd be back on Friday. She'd have to remind herself of that a few times this week. It wasn't forever. It was just until Friday.

Chapter Fourteen

❧✿❧

"**G**ood to have you back, Ransom."

Someone clapped him on the shoulder. Nate turned in the swivel chair to see James Henderson, 20-year veteran sportswriter for the *Duluth Herald*, settle his massive frame into the chair next to Nate's desk. Nate pushed his laptop to the side, leaning back to rest his feet on the top of his desk. No work got done when James decided to visit.

Nate leaned forward to grab his insulated mug. "Thanks. Make any headlines while I was gone?"

"Oh, you know me. They gave me a job writing them so I'd stop hogging the front page." James laughed at his own joke, his eyes all but disappearing above his cheeky face.

James and his big, boisterous family were all involved in the Duluth sports scene in some capacity. His father, a former head coach for the semipro Warriors football team, was a man so loved that when he passed away two years ago, the line of mourners at his visitation wrapped around a full city block trying to get into St. Peter's to pay respects. His two twin brothers, former d-linemen for UM-Duluth, joined the athletic department and still worked for the university. But James was the biggest star of the Henderson clan. He liked to play himself up to be as great as college hall of famer Pat Richter if you asked him. And there was no doubt James's future would have been as bright as a comet. But that was before he blew out his knee during training camp before his junior year as a Wisconsin Badger.

"So what did I miss around here? Anything?"

"Friday was Evelyn's last day. We catered in Moseby's," James said, rubbing his sizable belly.

Nate snapped his fingers. "I hate when I miss a free meal from Moseby's."

James lowered his voice and leaned forward. "And word on the street is you're taking another job. What's up with that?"

"Who told you that?"

James looked around the office, which was still pretty crowded even during the lunch hour. Across the room, the editorial staff met in the boardroom behind a wall of glass, mouths moving and hands gesturing wildly.

"Angi said someone called for you from some California magazine," he whispered.

"Seriously?" Nate sat upright, shuffling papers around on his desk, searching for a message he might have missed, buried in the pile of mail and interoffice memos he'd collected during the past two weeks. Angi Itura, office assistant for the features department, handed him everything in a small box that morning. He was still sorting through it.

"Tell me you're not leaving," James said with a frown that morphed his features into a houndlike expression.

"Wouldn't dream of it. This is just a freelance gig. I've been wanting to work with these guys forever if it's who I think it is."

"Good. I'd hate to see the only Brewers fan leave Duluth."

"No worries there, man."

Distracted, he searched through the stack again, and this time, found the yellow slip with "While You Were Out" at the top. Nate scanned the name and message, then waved it at James. "Got it. It's them."

James put his hands up. "I'll let you make that phone call then. Good luck." He pushed himself out of the seat. "Just think: I'll be able to say 'I knew him when he wrote for the *Duluth Herald*,'" he joked.

"I won't forget about you," he said to James's retreating back.

Nate fingered the yellow message, studying the name and phone number.

Coast Magazine. That piece he'd queried about illegal wildlife trafficking. It was a dream assignment—hot-button issue, something he was passionate about, lucrative pay. He couldn't believe it. Nate leaned back in his chair. Maybe he shouldn't get ahead of himself. They hadn't given him the go-ahead yet.

But a phone call and twenty minutes later, the story was his.

"Yes!" Nate pounded his fist on the desk, startling an intern named Jane at her desk. He mouthed "sorry" to her before he picked up his phone again and found Bethany's number in his contacts. She should be the first to hear his good news.

She picked up on the second ring.

"I thought you might be in class."

"Hi. No, just finished. How are you?" Bethany sounded like she was back to her usual cheerful self.

"I'm doing well. They missed me here. By the look of my mail and message pile anyway."

"Well, Hendricks misses you," she said, and Nate heard the pause in her breath. "I miss you."

"We'll have to do something about that. Friday is only three days away."

"That's three days too many," she said in a low voice.

"I'll make it up to you. You're free Friday, right?"

"Depends."

"On?"

"Your plans for us. I'm only up for one ice shack date per season."

He chuckled and leaned back, crossing his ankles on top his desk again. "What if we moved the blankets, hot chocolate, and good conversation inside this time?"

"That's more like it."

He cleared his throat. "So I have good news."

"Really? What's going on?"

He heard the jingle of keys and guessed she was leaving the studio.

"I got my dream assignment from a magazine I've wanted to write for for years."

"Dream assignment?"

"Yes. *Coast Magazine*. They're out of California."

"So you're quitting the newspaper?"

"No, this is freelance. I'll work on it in my spare time. Phone interviews, research, that sort of thing. Maybe a trip to San Francisco in March."

"There are worse places to be than California in the spring."

He wondered what he heard in her tone. The cheerfulness had faded into something more solemn. "What, no congratulations?" he said half-jokingly.

A few seconds of silence. "That's great, Nate. I'm happy for you."

All the right words, but not very convincing.

"Maybe we could swing the trip together? I've never been to San Francisco before. Have you?" He had no idea how long he'd need to be out there. At the moment, though, Nate wanted to hear that she liked the idea of traveling somewhere together.

"You'll be working. And I have classes, and Gran, and—"

"Humor me. Don't say no just yet, okay?"

"You're right. I'm kind of a buzzkill today. Sorry." He heard the smile back in her voice this time.

"No worries. You've had a lot on your mind." He put his feet on the floor and reached for a pen and notepad. *S'more stuff - hot chocolate mix - milk,* he wrote to remind himself of the Friday night necessities. He added "flowers" as an afterthought and grinned. She'd love flowers. Something unique, like her.

She sighed. "I miss you. Did I already say that?"

"Yes, but you can say it as many times as you'd like as far as I'm concerned."

"I'll stop at two. I don't want to be responsible for the inflated sense of self-importance you're sure to develop."

Nate shuffled his feet under the desk. "I'm humble to the core."

"Right," she said. "Well, I guess I'll see you on Friday."

He didn't want to say goodbye, but it was his first day back after a two-week absence. He didn't want anyone calling him out as a slacker. "You're right, you know."

"I'm right about what?"

"It is three days too many."

Bethany laughed, a throaty, sexy sound. Nate clamped his lips shut when he caught himself growling under his breath, something he probably shouldn't do in a crowded newsroom.

"Did you just growl?" she asked incredulously.

He smiled. "That was my stomach. Lunch hour, you know?"

"See you, Ransom."

Friday wouldn't come soon enough.

Chapter Fifteen

Bethany finished putting the last of the dishes away before loading the dirty ones into Gran's dishwasher. She glanced out the window above the sink as she wiped down the counter. It had been another gray day, but now in the hour before last light, a pink tinge colored the sky above the line of barren lilac bushes at the rear of the property. She stretched over the sink to see beyond Gran's fence and toward the lake, to the luminous bands of pink, lavender, and tangerine painted on the horizon.

"What's so interesting out there?" asked Gran, still sitting at the table with her coffee.

"Oh, nothing. Just a pretty sky." Bethany straightened and closed the dishwasher. It grumbled to life when she pushed the button.

"My pretty sky days are numbered, so I appreciate every one of them."

Bethany turned away from the window, groaning. "I don't like it when you talk that way."

Gran waved away her comment. "Don't get all delicate with me." She drained her mug and held it out for a refill. "It's inevitable."

"I know that, Gran. I don't live in a fantasy world. But between you joking about dying all the time, and Mom and Dad not even bothering to come after your ER visit, well, it's just too much." She replaced the carafe on the coffeepot and handed the steaming mug back to Gran, chancing a look. She'd raised her voice, something she never did to Gran, and it had an effect, that was clear. For once, Gran was silent. Her expression spoke of understanding and, amazingly enough, a little guilt.

"You're right. I'm sorry."

Bethany put her hand to her ear. "What was that?"

"Yes, that was your crusty grandmother apologizing. Don't rub it in."

Bethany laughed and stood behind Gran, hugging her shoulders. "You're so lucky I love you."

Gran patted the side of Bethany's face. "And you're so lucky that I put up with you."

Bethany heard the gate squeak on its rusty hinges in the backyard. There was nothing wrong with Gran's hearing either.

"That'd be your honey, wouldn't it? Better get out there to meet him before he wanders in here and sees me in my long johns."

Bethany stepped back and looked down at Gran. "But you're not wearing long johns."

Gran rolled her eyes. "I know that. That's code for 'hurry up' because I don't want to see anybody."

Laughing, she kissed Gran on the cheek, grabbed her coat off the hook, and dashed outside before Nate even latched the gate behind him. He didn't notice her coming out the back door until she called to him.

"Hey there."

Nate lit up when he saw her, and Bethany melted. His was not so much a movie star face, with eyes a little too solemn, a nose more pinched than the standard, and a full set of lips with a natural downward turn at the corners. But the effect when he did smile was that of the sun breaking through the clouds, and she couldn't help smiling herself.

Bethany hugged him tightly, burying her nose in his coat collar, breathing in the heady combination of woodsmoke and cologne. He bowed his head into her hair.

"Missed you," she whispered. Why was he holding his other arm out of sight? Bethany narrowed her eyes when he moved it farther out of reach. "You have something behind your back, don't you?"

Nate drew back, surprised. "What makes you think that?"

"You're only hugging me with one arm." Again, she tried to see behind his back, but almost lost her footing on the snow-covered path instead.

"Before you kill us both, I'll concede," he said, handing her a bouquet of yellow tea roses, carnations, freesia, and one large Asiatic lily. "I also have the makings for s'mores since you're going to ask me next what's in the bag."

"I'm not good at waiting for surprises."

"I know. I remember how you bugged me the night we went to the ice shack."

"'Bugged' you? Interesting choice of words."

Nate hugged her tight while they made their way to Bethany's door. "Like a love bug."

Bethany nudged him in the ribs. "Good save."

Inside, Bethany got a fire blazing in the wood stove in no time. Nate helped her pull the loveseat closer to the stove, and then she draped a quilted throw around their shoulders as she settled in next to him.

Nate opened up the package of graham crackers, then the chocolate, and deftly assembled one chocolate-covered cracker, then another. Bethany held the stainless steel skewer for him to load with marshmallows. Then Nate took over, opening the stove door, letting the heat work its magic.

They sat in silence for a minute, watching the marshmallows turn golden. Bethany studied his profile as he leaned toward the fire. The flames cast a glow on his features. She could hardly look away.

"How's your grandmother?" he asked with a sideways glance.

"She told me tonight that she's dying."

Nate's eyes widened. "She what?"

"You heard right." Bethany crossed her arms, still watching the fire. "That's her idea of a joke."

"Not really funny, especially after last weekend," he said, drawing the skewer away from the flames. He squeezed each marshmallow between two crackers, then added some chocolate chips. As the chocolate melted, he handed one of the plates to Bethany.

"She has a morbid sense of humor."

"I'll say." He put a s'more on his plate, then rested the skewer on the mosaic tile underneath the stove. "Why is that?"

Bethany blew on her s'more, but it was still too hot. She set the plate on her lap. "Gran likes getting a reaction. It used to be she just wanted to make me laugh. Now she goes for shock value."

"Maybe you're not giving her enough attention," Nate said around a mouthful of graham cracker and marshmallow. A dark smudge of chocolate decorated his face, lip to chin.

Bethany let out a short, barking laugh, startling Silda, who lounged on the uppermost level of her cat tree in the corner. After one swish of her tail and a withering look, Silda decided nothing was too out of the ordinary and went back to napping.

Bethany shook her head. "That's funny. Actually, it's not. That's the source of a lot of my anxiety this week." She looked again at Nate. "Are you going to take care of the chocolate on your face, or do I have to?"

Nate set his plate carefully on the table, leaned back against the couch, stretching his long legs in front of him and his arms over the back. He was the epitome of leisurely hotness, chocolate smudge notwithstanding.

"I'm pretty sure you'll do a better job of getting rid of it than I will," he said in a low voice.

She leaned forward and slowly kissed away the chocolate spot on the bottom of his chin, inching closer to his lips as she followed the sweet trail on his skin. Then Bethany drew away for a second.

"Why does it taste better on your face than on the s'more?"

Nate's eyes were closed. "I'm sure there's a scientific explanation. Can't think about that at the moment," he murmured.

She inhaled the chocolate-rich scent of his breath as they touched foreheads. "Remind me to look it up when we're finished here."

"You're a long way from finished. Come here."

His lips found hers as he wrapped both arms around her. She couldn't help the sharp intake of breath from the force of his kiss as he wove his fingers into her hair. Bethany couldn't get close enough to him. The sensation was almost too much.

Bethany pulled away a minute later, her lips tender. She sighed. "I'm glad you came over. I needed something good to happen."

Nate sat up. "You seem to be in a better mood than when I talked with you Tuesday," he said, tucking her hair behind an ear.

"I think it's the prospect of the weekend. Of seeing you." She shook her head. "It was a tough week."

"Do you want to talk about it?"

"Not really. I don't know. I mean, a lot of it is Gran. And other things."

"'Other things' like?"

Bethany stared at the flames dancing inside the stove. A familiar tightness crept into her chest when she thought of the last few days, the heated conversations over the phone with her mother, and then the last one with her father. After last weekend, Dad promised he'd make the trip to see Gran. But then client meetings ran overtime, one of his paralegals quit unexpectedly, and the research needed for an upcoming case took more time than he'd planned. It was a different excuse for each day that week.

"Parents. As usual."

Nate's silence was an invitation for more she knew, but again, she couldn't go there. Her thoughts were one thing, articulating them was quite another.

"Did you see them this week? Did they come to see your grandmother?"

Bethany huffed. "Are you kidding? Marconi, Marconi and Dietrich can't survive without them for a day. Not even for his mother."

"I'm sorry." Nate reached for her hand, his thumb caressing hers.

Bethany shrugged. "I shouldn't be surprised. They never had time for their kid. Why would it be different for Gran?"

The beat of silence that followed hung between them like an iron pendulum. She pushed her hair off her forehead and rested her elbows on her knees.

He looked over at her with serious eyes. "Funny that your dad is like that when your Gran is the opposite, from what you tell me at least."

"Yeah. I have no idea how *that* happened."

"Are your parents that way with each other? With showing affection?"

Bethany shook her head slowly while she picked at her fingernail.

Again, a weighted pause filled the air. Bethany groaned. She felt cornered into giving more of an explanation.

"All my life my parents led these completely separate lives—really successful ones—but they were so career obsessed and on the go, that we never seemed like a family. It was always me and Gran at home, doing the family things —meals, getting me ready for school, then homework help at night. Then we turned into a commuter family, them in Minneapolis, me and Gran staying in town. Only seeing them on the weekends. That's my world view of marriage, of being a couple. I don't want that."

Nate touched her hand. His soulful eyes stared at their intertwined fingers. "That's understandable," he said quietly.

Bethany had made him feel uncomfortable. He seemed at a loss for words, but she didn't blame him. Even after all these years, she could hear the resentment in her own voice. It was a turnoff for some people. She'd always been so good at keeping that part of herself off limits. What was wrong with her?

Nate shifted in his spot so he faced her. "What do you want?"

"What do you mean?"

"You just told me what marriage shouldn't be. What's your ideal?"

She leaned her head against the back of the couch, trying to piece her thoughts together. What did she want? So many times she'd noted the details about her parents' marriage she didn't like that she'd never considered what she wished for if she was lucky enough to find someone worthy of a long-term commitment.

"I liked the way my friends' parents did marriage. That stability seemed perfect. Movie nights together, shuttling kids to games, eating big Saturday breakfasts at the dining room table. Big, rowdy, talky times together."

He nodded and let out an abrupt laugh. "That sounds like my parents."

"Tell me about them."

He looked out the window. "Married thirty-three years. They still hold hands in public. I've never heard either one say an unkind word about the other, at least not in front of us kids. Best friends."

Bethany sighed. "I love that. Did you guys do the big Saturday breakfasts together? Pancakes and bacon? Egg casseroles and fruit compotes?"

"Fruit *what*?"

"Compotes. It's like fruit in a sugary syrup."

Nate's brow wrinkled. "All of the above except the compote things."

Bethany massaged a spot on her shoulder, trying to rub away the tension that had knotted there during the last few days. When Nate noticed, he gently pushed her hand aside to take over.

He blew the air out of his cheeks. "Maybe this isn't the time to bring it up, but—"

Bethany inhaled when he paused. She didn't like the sound of it.

"Sometimes I get the feeling that our relationship,

or the direction I hope we're headed anyway, is somehow dependent on your relationship with your parents."

She felt him studying her. Bethany stared straight ahead, chewing on her lip.

"I mean, you've admitted that you date, but no one ever seriously."

"That's right. So?" She didn't really want to expand on it. Maybe it was the week's woes that weighed her down. Or maybe it was the subject of her parents, of expectations that propelled her desire to shut off the conversation, to move on to lighter topics.

"So you seem to have an insecurity about getting close to people," he said, moving his hand from her shoulder to touch a strand of her hair, twirl it around his finger. "To me."

"That's surprising?"

"No, considering your family's dynamics. But maybe it's time to work through it."

She mentally shrugged away the discussion.

Nate's brows dipped. "What does that mean?"

Bethany looked at him. "What?"

"You shook your head."

"I did? I guess I'm just not ready to talk about that."

"By 'that' you mean us?"

Bethany leaned forward to open the door of the stove, and throw another log into it. She rearranged the other logs with the fire poker, thankful for the excuse to not look him the eye. "Yes."

When Bethany glanced back, he sat there with a tight

smile on his face. His smile broadened, but the hurt was still evident.

"Nate, I'm sorry. I don't know what else to say."

"My time is almost up, isn't it?" He twisted the marshmallow bag closed, brushed crumbs into his palm, and emptied them into the plastic bag on the floor. The smile was still there, but it didn't reach his eyes.

"Huh?"

"This is when you usually call it quits on a relationship. It was a big joke when it came up during the night of our second date, but that's the truth. Three to four weeks. Things start getting a little twitchy." His hand found her shoulder again, rubbing it gently.

Bethany clutched the poker handle until her knuckles whitened. "I wasn't even thinking about that before you brought it up." This was getting out of control. Why was he being so confrontational? She pushed the log farther back into the stove, turning it over again. A shower of sparks erupted inside. "You're asking an awful lot of me after the week I just had."

He dropped his hand from her shoulder. At the same time, a few sparks flew onto the tile when the already smoldering wood shifted. Bethany tamped them out with the quilted fire glove next to the tools. Heat washed over her face. Too uncomfortable to bear, she turned away.

Nate paused. His chin dropped to his chest. "You're right. I'm sorry."

Bethany set down the glove and leaned back into the couch, into his arm. She kissed him lightly, then snuggled her face into his shoulder. "It's all right."

"No, it's not. I have no right to make any demands. It was wrong."

She threw her arm around his chest, hugging him tight in response. His breath was in her hair.

He continued. "When I saw you at the studio again for the first time in seventeen years, it was like the schoolboy crush all over again. But it was more, much more. I feel a connection to you, Bethany. That's not something I take lightly."

Bethany nudged him in the ribs. "You say that to all your dates, I bet."

He drew away from her. Even before he spoke, she knew that wasn't true.

"You're more than just a 'date.' You're smart, witty, ambitious. You care deeply. I can see that in how you talk about your grandmother. You see things through a different lens than a lot of people," he said, looking down at his hands. "And I have to say, when you walk into a room, people shut up because—"

"—I'm usually the loudest one there."

—because you're stop-the-heart beautiful."

Bethany looked down at her shoes, self-conscious. It wasn't that she hadn't heard variations of those words a dozen times, coming from an equal number of guys she'd dated over the years. It was the way Nate spoke them. Heartfelt and to the point. He wasn't saying them to win her over.

"Thank you. That's the nicest compliment I've ever had."

"Really? I find that hard to believe."

"Maybe it's because you're a writer. You know exactly

how to string words together to get the right reaction." She struggled to keep a straight face, but when the uncertainly registered on his features, Bethany broke down. "You are so gullible. I'm not even slightly serious."

He leaned over and touched his forehead to hers. "It's because I have a lot at stake," he whispered.

Bethany kissed him, nibbling at his lip.

That simple action ignited the spark in Nate's gaze. He slipped his arm around her shoulders, pulling her against him and let his mouth graze hers in an unhurried kiss. Even as she smiled against his lips and let desire wash over her, a nagging thought entered Bethany's mind.

What if she had a lot at stake too and didn't realize what it was until it was too late?

Chapter Sixteen

N ate couldn't have slept any worse than if his mattress were ply board and he had a rock for a pillow. His thoughts kept running on repeat until well past midnight, and the cot he'd brought from home was more suited to camping trips. The creaks of the metal frame when he shifted his weight echoed in the empty bedroom of his grandmother's house, keeping him and probably Jana, who slept in the room next to his, awake.

Bethany, of course, was the source of his sleeplessness.

Though they'd parted with a kiss goodnight and plans to see each at the auction, the impression Nate was left with after saying goodbye to Bethany last night was that they were on borrowed time. Her track record with long-term relationships spoke for itself.

He laid in bed thinking until the skeletal branches outside his window began to reveal their shapes in the predawn light. Padding into the kitchen, he fried himself an egg to slap between two wheat slices and a piece of cheddar, and sat in the near dark eating and listening to the coffeepot gurgle in the corner.

There wasn't much more he could do to prove he was sincere. Bethany called the shots from here on out.

Nate chewed over bits of their conversation for the next two hours until he and Jana arrived at Del's Auction House. The more he stewed, the more he worried. Even the presale hustle at the auction house wasn't enough to get him out of his contemplative mood. He found a Styrofoam cup of coffee to nurse while he hung at the back of the room to watch the rest of his grandmother's earthly possessions be re-homed during the next four hours.

"Hey there."

The voice startled Nate.

It was Paige Goff.

Leaning against the pillar, Nate hadn't seen her coming around the other side. He braced himself. She looked a little too bright-eyed for his mood.

"Good morning, Paige." He took a sip of his coffee and his gaze returned to the room.

"You have a good turnout. Should be a lucrative day."

"Hope so." Nate wondered what excuse he could use to extract himself from the conversation and Paige's company. "Is the local auction house on your list of photos to get for the North Shore feature?"

"Not really. I was actually on the pier this morning getting some shots. Saw the crowd, so I thought I'd wander over." Paige swept her hair behind her shoulder, returning her attention to Nate. "By the way, congratulations on your new assignment," she said, a hint of a smile curving her lips. "That's a big win for your clip file."

He looked at her. "Big win? I have no idea what that means."

She threw her hands up. "The assignment for *Coast*. It's huge, though I probably don't need to tell you that."

His confusion momentarily tied his tongue. How did she know? Had he mentioned querying the magazine when he met her? There was no way he would have done that.

Paige's eyebrows pinched together as she laughed.

"Don't look so surprised. Magazine publishing circles run pretty small, especially for people like us who tend to work on the same types of projects."

Nate was still stunned. It felt so intrusive. How did she know?

Paige laid her hand on his arm. "I didn't mean to embarrass you. I just wanted to acknowledge the accomplishment."

"Thank you, but I'm not embarrassed. It surprises me that you know something I thought was personal."

"I don't blame you. I do a lot of work for *Coast*. My parents live in Monterey, so I spend a good amount of time there and have a large catalog of photos from the area. I'm an easy contact for the editors if they need something quickly."

"So the editors readily share who's queried them?" Nate didn't try to hide his annoyance. "That's interesting."

Paige leaned in close. "Tim, the acquisitions editor, and I actually dated. We still talk. He saw that you were in Duluth and asked if I knew you."

"I see."

"Really, Nate. I'm sorry. I shouldn't have brought it up."

Nate relaxed. "It's fine. Early mornings don't agree with me. I'm a little testy."

Paige's brows shot up. "I hear you there."

As Del prepared to start the auction, Bethany walked through the front door, looking flustered. Not that it made him feel any better, but she looked like she'd lost a few winks during the night too. She scanned the room once, then again, until she found him. She stood on her tiptoes and waved, then weaved through the crowd toward him. As Bethany got closer, she slowed, a look of irritation clouding her face. She'd noticed Paige.

Bethany sidled right up to him and planted a big, fat kiss on his lips. Even as they kissed, her eyes crinkled with amusement, like she knew this was her game and Paige wasn't invited to play. His pulse probably registered on the Richter scale, he mused, as Bethany pulled away. And her smug look as she acknowledged Paige didn't escape his attention.

Nate scratched his jaw, wondering how he got lucky enough to get them both together. He pushed away from the pole. "Bethany, do you know Paige Goff?"

"Of course. We met at the Lodge, right? You're Sean and Darcy's friend," said Bethany, her voice an octave higher than usual.

"Yes, that's right." Her finger pointed between him and Bethany. "And you two are...dating?"

Bethany looped her arm around Nate's and looked up at him. "Are we?" she asked with that same amused expression. She didn't wait for him to answer before she turned back to Paige. "Yes, for a couple months now."

Nate raised his eyebrows at Bethany's fabrication of an extra month added to their relationship, but Bethany didn't look at him again. Instead, she pulled up one of the chairs from the back row and sat down. That grin again, the mischievous one.

"So, are you still working on the photos for the North Shore feature? I thought you would have left town a while ago." Bethany grimaced. "I can't imagine auction house photos would be very exciting for a travel article."

Paige stepped back and looked around, like she wanted to be somewhere else. Of course he wouldn't mind in the least if she took up space in another part of room. But then her gaze rested on Bethany again.

"No, I didn't plan to take photos of the auction house. Just didn't have anything better to do this morning. Thought I'd check it out." She crossed her arms. "Say, I see someone over by the concessions. I'll talk to you later, Nate." Paige glanced at Bethany and wiggled her fingers. "Bye now."

"Good riddance," Bethany mumbled.

Nate glanced at Bethany, enjoying what seemed like jealousy. "What, you're not friends?"

She looked at him with a deadpan expression. Bethany stood and leaned into him.

"How are you doing this morning?"

He held up his coffee. "If it wasn't for this, I'd be asleep against this pole."

"It's probably a little strange to see people handling your grandmother's things."

Nate rubbed his neck, trying to smooth out the knot of tension from sleeplessness. "Not really. My family has everything that was important to her. To us. Some of the furniture. The few pieces of jewelry. A lot of her art."

"Like the bird sculptures. I love those."

"Yes, the birds. Those are priceless."

"Probably even more so if you ever find any more pairs."

He stared at her, a question that he meant to ask her popping back into his head at that moment. About the birds, the flicker sculpture. He opened his mouth to do just that, but the look on her face stopped him cold. Bethany's slack-jawed expression was one of disbelief. Or anger. Maybe both.

"Bethany?" He looked in the general direction that held her attention, but the mass of people didn't yield any clues.

She made a guttural sound. "I can't believe this."

"What is it?"

Bethany turned to him, grim-faced.

"My mother is here."

Chapter Seventeen

Bethany uncrossed her arms and left Nate's side, striding purposefully through the crowd, undeterred by whomever was in her path. As people saw her coming, they simply stepped back as she made her way to the front door on the opposite side of the large warehouse. Good thing. Mowing people down was a distinct possibility.

Inside the auction house, Lillian Marconi was a diamond among stones—flashy, cold, totally out of place. She stood just inside the door, wearing her trademark sleek leather duster with a brown Burberry scarf. Even from across the room, Bethany could feel the disdain radiating from her mother like icy tendrils. Whatever her mother's reason was for showing up unexpectedly at the auction house could not be a pleasant one. With each step, Bethany's heart beat like a tribal drum until she was sure it would pound itself into exhaustion.

Then Lillian spotted Bethany. Technically, Lillian didn't wave at her. It was more of a finger in the air, like a gesture meant to signal a waiter, and it just added to Bethany's irritation. She didn't like feeling as if she were being summoned.

Bethany stopped within an arm's length of Lillian.

"Somehow I missed the call that let me know you were coming. And here of all places."

Lillian looked to the ceiling and heaved a sigh, her version of an eye roll. "It slipped my mind. I didn't have time."

"Really? The Twin Cities to Hendricks is almost a four-hour trip." Lillian's *modus operandi* for visits leaned heavily on the element of surprise these days, though Bethany could count on one hand the times her mother graced Bethany with her presence during the last few years.

Lillian glanced over Bethany's shoulder to the noisy auction house and the people milling around the tables until her gaze rested on Bethany again. "Listen. I'd like to go outside and have a chat. This isn't the place for what I have to say."

"I don't see why it makes a difference where we talk."

"*Bethany.*"

Without a word, Bethany walked past her mother and pushed through the front door. Despite the temperature outside, she was on fire. Her mother's presumptuousness was out of line. On the sidewalk, she turned around and waited.

"Did you come to see Gran? Finally?"

Lillian gave her a warning look. "I have seen your grandmother, yes, and your father is still with her."

"So what does your coming to town have to do with me?"

Lillian rubbed her butter-smooth gloves together, looking down at them with her jaw firmly set.

"I wanted to let you know how decidedly unhappy I am, *we* are, about our conversations this week. The accusatory tone, the ranting."

"I hardly ranted. And I already got the message loud and clear that both of you weren't happy with me calling you out." Lillian scolded her for her behavior? Amazing.

"We were overwhelmed these last eight days. We simply couldn't get away."

"Yes, we all know the firm would simply die without you. Meanwhile, Gran was being treated for stroke symptoms."

Lillian's thin lips pressed together as she studied Bethany. "That's not fair and you know it."

"No. You know what's not fair? It's pushing your kid off on your mother-in-law to raise. And expecting your kid to take on the caregiver role when Gran ends up in the hospital. Not that I mind because Gran is all I have and she did the same for me. But think about Gran's feelings for once. Her own son can't bother to see her after a pretty critical medical emergency."

"Your grandmother knows how important she is to us, and our limitations."

Bethany pressed her fingertips against her temple, resigned. "Great. What else?"

Lillian's shoulders dropped slightly like one of her burdens lifted. "There is something else, something you probably won't like very much."

Bethany snorted humorlessly. "As if anything you have to say fills me with—"

"Enough."

Bethany inhaled through her nostrils, steeling herself.

"We think it's best to encourage Don—your grandmother to sell the house and move near us. To a retirement facility."

Her mother's words floated around her, not making sense at first. Sell the house. Move. Retirement facility. When it finally dawned on her what Lillian meant, Bethany was speechless.

Lillian must have taken her silence as a willingness to listen further. She continued in her robotic, matter-of-fact tone.

"Your father and I are going to take her back with us for the week. I scheduled appointments with admission directors at three retirement communities during the next few days. We're going to tour them, ask questions, let your grandmother get a feel for what she might like."

"So, a nursing home."

"Not a nursing home. A retirement—"

"Yeah, yeah. I heard what you said. But what it really means is you want to stick her somewhere unfamiliar, without friends or family—"

Lillian put one gloved finger in the air. "We're her family."

"No." Bethany shook her head, staring at her mother. "You don't get to do this."

"Excuse me?"

"I like Gran here. I'm pretty sure she feels the same way."

Lillian took a step closer, near enough that Bethany noticed the scent of lilac soap and the faint spider veins on her mother's chin underneath the layer of makeup.

"This is not open for discussion. Your grandmother is spending the week with us. Then we'll bring her back next Sunday. At that point, we'll talk about next steps."

"Right. And meanwhile I'm here."

"You're an adult, Bethany. You can handle it."

Bethany couldn't believe what she was hearing. "Wait. Do you think this is about my fear of being alone?"

Lillian gave her an arched look. "Why are you almost thirty and still living with your grandmother?"

Incredulous, Bethany studied Lillian for a long moment, wondering how the person standing before her could be her mother, how she could speak with such thoughtlessness.

"I can't believe you just said that."

Lillian stared at her, lips pressed together. "I'm not sure what other reason it could be."

The heat of Bethany's anger evaporated the moisture that threatened to dampen her eyes. There was no sign that what her mother said was only a heat-of-the-moment reaction. On the contrary, what Lillian said, Lillian meant. And she never apologized, no matter how cutting her words might be. But instead of letting her mother's remarks carve away a sliver of her self-esteem yet again, something shifted inside her. This time Bethany knew the little spark of affection she had for her parents had finally been snuffed out.

As Bethany turned away to walk to her car, she waited for the sorrow to come. But instead, there was a hollowness. It was too late for sorrow. Instead, she was overcome with something else that surprised her—a flicker of relief.

SHE DROVE AROUND THE BLOCK TO HER STUDIO, unlocked the door, and kicked off her snow boots on the mat behind the counter. The silence of the space without the lights on lent a peaceful stillness to the whirlwind inside her mind. Bethany padded to the center of the room, shucking her coat, her sweater, and her socks in a colorful trail behind her. Sitting on the mat, Bethany focused on the quiet.

Tears weren't usually part of her emotional repertoire, but they suddenly came. Bethany stretched out on her back, staring at the ceiling, alternating between resting her hands at her sides while in a butterfly pose, and swiping at the wet trail that ran from her eyes into her ears. She was more angry than anything, angry that her parents wanted to control Gran and her when they'd lived harmoniously together all these years. Angry that her mother and father viewed her as dependent still, despite Bethany owning her own business, splitting living expenses with Gran, paying off her college loans.

A knock on the door startled her. Abruptly, Bethany sat up and looked to the front of the studio.

Ethan.

He stood at the front door, both hands planted on either side of his face, peering into the darkened space. He waved when he saw her.

Shoot. She wanted to be alone.

Reluctantly, she waved back, and got up, taking advantage of the distance across the room to wipe away the remnants of tears. As soon as she unlocked the door, Ethan barged in.

"Why are laying in the middle of your studio in the dark? You looked dead." His eyes narrowed when he looked closely at her. "Are you crying?"

Bethany groaned. "No. Yes." She waved her hands with frustration. "Not anymore." She walked back to her spot on the mat, with Ethan following close behind.

They sat down together, almost hip to hip. Ethan ducked his head to see her face. "Want to talk about it?"

She hugged her knees to her chest, resting her chin on one. "Not really."

Ethan prodded her with his foot. "I'm a good listener."

Bethany straightened her legs in front of her. "I know you are." She sighed and let a minute or so pass while she tried to collect her thoughts. Then she turned to him.

"Do I seem like a needy person to you?"

He frowned. "Needy?"

Bethany nodded.

"Well, you do have a tendency to take more than your fair share of candy from the container at the register when you come in, but—"

She whacked his arm. "I do not. Be serious. Am I needy?"

Ethan laughed and put his arm around her shoulders. "Bethany, you're a successful, independent, pull-no-punches kind of gal. Of course you're not needy. Where is this coming from?"

She gave him a sidelong glance. "I had an...interesting morning."

"Go on."

"My parents are in town visiting my grandmother." She rubbed her cheeks again.

Ethan huffed. "Well, finally, right?"

"No kidding. Anyway, my mother said I was needy because I live with my grandmother."

"Ouch."

"Yeah."

Ethan looked at his shoes, retied one of the laces. "Living with your grandmother doesn't mean you are needy. It means you and her have a mutually beneficial situation. Needy people take advantage."

Bethany fell back on the mat and threw an arm over her face.

"And now they want to move her to the Twin Cities into a retirement place."

"Seriously? That's so wrong."

"And they're taking her back today—oh!"

Bethany sprang to her feet and fished out her phone from the coat pocket. She dialed Gran, listened to the steady ringing. No answer. She had to get back home before they left, though she knew her being there wouldn't change their course of action. Far from it. They could already be gone for all she knew. Grabbing the trail of clothes, Bethany threw them on and stuffed her feet back into the boots.

"I need to go before they leave town."

"Of course. Want me to drive?"

Bless his heart, Ethan wanted to help. But really, Bethany just wanted to be alone.

"No, thank you. I don't want to subject you to my family drama."

Ethan held the front door open for her, and she slipped out, then locked the door behind her.

"It's not a problem."

She put her hand up. "I'm serious. I'll be all right."

"Call if you need anything—a shoulder to cry on, candy from the jar on the counter—"

Bethany chuckled softly in spite of the sourness that sat at the back of her throat. "I will," she called over her shoulder as she hurried toward her car.

Chapter Eighteen

Nate lost sight of Bethany when she left through the front door with her mother, and after thirty minutes when she didn't return, he decided to go looking for her. Del Arbuckle and his sales team had everything under control anyway. The only reason Nate showed up was to get out with Jana after being stuck packing for the last three weeks inside his grandmother's house. No one would miss him.

It was a cloudless morning, which looked harmless enough inside the warm auction house until Nate stepped outside. The bitter wind sliced through his canvas coat like a steel blade. He stood his collar up to cover his ears, but it was a poor substitute for a hat. Squinting as the wind pried tears from his eyes, he scanned the parking lot for Bethany's car. It was nowhere in sight. He fished his phone out of his pocket, called her number, but the phone went straight to voicemail.

Nate sensed trouble. Aside from Bethany's reaction to her mother, there was something else brewing. Their conversation last night still nagged him. Maybe he should check if Bethany went home. He could clear the air by apologizing again for pushing her for a commitment, tell her he'd let her take the next step. Yes, that was what he'd do.

He stopped for scones from Debi's Donuts, and a few minutes later, pulled alongside the curb at Bethany's house.

But her car wasn't there either.

For a few minutes, Nate sat in the car, warm currents from the heater brushing his face, wondering what to do. Write her a note on the bag with "Call Me" on it? Check the yoga studio? Maybe she was at Two Tree with her mother. They might have gone there to talk.

No, he wouldn't do any of those things.

Nate unbuckled himself, grabbed the scones and got out of the car. He walked along the fence to the front of the house—Donna's house—and knocked on her front door.

If Bethany wasn't here, then he'd visit Donna. He should check on how she was coming along since her ER visit anyway, but he couldn't deny the ulterior motive he had in mind either.

Donna opened the door wearing a knee-length quilted robe and wide smile.

"My day has just been made. A handsome man bearing a Debi's Donuts bag is at my door. Come in." She stepped aside and let him enter. "Although I have no idea why you're coming to the front door. All the people I like come to the back door."

Nate chuckled. "I'll keep that in mind."

"Bethany isn't here in case you're wondering."

"Yes, I didn't see her car. But I thought I'd check in on you, see how you're holding up." He followed her into the kitchen and pulled out a chair at the table when she pointed to the seat opposite her. It looked like she'd been poring over cookbooks. A small pile was scattered across the tabletop, a recipe card half-written beside them. A lit candle gave off a thin wisp of black smoke that dissipated as he sat down. "So how are you?"

She pushed a stray curl from her eyes. "Frankly, I'm dying."

Nate froze, unsure of what to say. He remembered Bethany mentioning her penchant for saying such things, but nonetheless it caught him off guard.

"But I plan on dying young as far into the future as possible." Donna guffawed and slapped the table. "Your face! I'm sorry. It's the Marconi humor."

Nate exhaled. "It's too early in the day for that. Did Bethany tell you I'm an easy mark or something?"

"She didn't need to. You have that earnest look about you." Donna reached for the Debi's bag that sat between them and peered in. "Which one is for me?"

Nate leaned back. "Whichever one you'd like. There's a lemon blueberry, chocolate chip, and a low-fat cranberry orange in there."

"Low-fat. Let me guess: that one's for me. Darned arteries," she said, taking it out of the bag. "Thank you."

"You're welcome. Low-fat or not, don't tell Bethany I'm bringing you sweets. She'll have my head."

"Your secret is safe," she said, sampling the scone and rolled her eyes. "Debi is some kind of mastermind, isn't she? Would you like coffee? Help yourself," she offered, nodding to the coffeemaker on the counter.

Nate poured himself some and sat back down.

Her eyes narrowed when she glanced again at him. "So what's the real reason you're here? An old woman's health shouldn't be your only concern."

Nate clutched his chest in mock horror. "That hurts."

Donna's brows lifted and she circled the rim of her cup with her finger. "Fine. I won't totally dismiss the gesture. But it's a curious thing that you waited until Bethany left before you showed up."

She was sharper than he bargained for. Nate raised his hand in surrender. "Guilty. You Marconi women are a hard lot."

Donna smiled. "To your detriment."

Nate hesitated. It was not the time to second-guess himself, sitting at the kitchen table with Donna Marconi, bribing her with Debi's Donuts. But he couldn't help it. If Bethany found out that he'd come to see Donna with the intention of asking why her granddaughter seemed so standoffish lately, well, Nate knew how fast Bethany would show him the door. But Nate needed to know where he stood, what Bethany might be thinking, and if they had a chance. He was getting desperate.

"Bethany's been quiet lately. When I try talking to her, it's like she's filtering everything she says."

She shook her head slightly and sighed. "She's a pill,

that one. Like a walnut. A shell as hard as the dickens, but once you crack it open, look out."

Nate chuckled. "I don't know about the pill part, but she's pretty special."

"Warm, generous to a fault sometimes, loves to joke." Donna shook her head. "But she can also be bullheaded and selfish. A true Gemini."

"I wouldn't have guessed she was anything but warm and generous."

Donna's words contradicted the impression he'd formed of Bethany in the last month. He'd seen her warmth firsthand in the way she talked about Donna, with the students who came into her studio, and with Darcy as Bethany helped her friend plan the gala. She definitely wasn't the in-his-face grade-school diva he remembered from years ago.

Donna got up to rinse out her mug. "It's a trust thing that keeps her from opening up. If she doesn't think you have her back, forget it. She needs to know a person is going to stick around before she invests her time and energy. Doesn't want anyone stealing her heart."

"Where does that come from?" He knew the answer, but wanted Donna's take on it.

She pursed her lips slightly. "Her parents were always attorneys first and parents second. I'm not casting blame. I guess if I was, I'd have to look in the mirror first. I raised her father, after all. Bethany was a very needy, insecure child because of their...living situation."

Nate wrapped his fingers around the warm mug. "She

doesn't seem like that now though. She's confident, funny, smart."

"When she's happy, my granddaughter can be the most charismatic and charming person you'll meet. My guess is she's backing off because she knows your time here isn't permanent."

"Makes sense."

"She's afraid of getting burned."

Nate watched the candle flame flicker, thinking. He took a sip of coffee and gazed across the table at Donna, then set the mug down.

"We were at the auction house this morning. She left in a hurry. Her mother showed up."

Donna rolled her eyes. "They both came this morning, her mother and father. Who knows where Peter went to. Lillian flew off to confront Bethany about how she got in their face this week for not checking on me," Donna said, frowning. "Oh boy, I can't imagine the fireworks that went off when those two got together."

Nate leaned back in the chair. "Yeah, Bethany was pretty upset just seeing her there."

"Lillian tends to have that effect on a lot of people." She popped the last bite of scone in her mouth and finished chewing. "You know, if it's any consolation, you're only the second one who's ever made it past the threshold here twice. That's saying something."

"Who was the first?"

"Some string bean track star in high school. Can't even remember his name." She waved her hand, dismissing the memory.

Nate stretched out his legs under the table, wondering if he and Bethany would have dated in high school or if she still would have avoided him even then. He was kind of a string bean himself as a teen. "Well, I think me being allowed inside speaks more for your hospitality than Bethany's feelings for me."

Donna wore an amused expression, the skin around her eyes crinkling, enhancing their blueness. The older woman's fine-boned features were offset by a full head of white wavy hair and coupled with her life-of-the-party demeanor, Nate guessed she was quite the heart-stopper in her younger days, just like her granddaughter was now.

"Maybe you're right, but Bethany is an easy read in some sense," Donna said. "She doesn't usually tell me much about the guys she dates. I dare call them boyfriends with as fast as they're in and out of her life. But I have heard a lot about you. That's something."

Nate laughed then gritted his teeth. He paused. "Still. If she hasn't had any long-term relationships, I guess it doesn't bode well for me."

"Shouldn't you be talking with her about these things?"

Guilt ate at Nate for pressing Donna. "We have talked. Just looking for your input."

"Bethany has never been lacking for male attention, that's for sure. But no, she hasn't dated anyone seriously. At least not that I can remember, even when she lived in Marquette." She grimaced. "I guess your chances of sticking around are slim."

Nate struggled to keep a neutral expression. He didn't like the idea of another guy enjoying Bethany's company.

"She seems to like reeling them in, then letting them go before they get too comfortable."

If Donna made one more reference to Bethany's distaste for commitments, he might throw up his hands and walk out the door. But wasn't that what he came looking for? Donna was a straight shooter, maybe a little too candid. She'd tell him if he was wasting his time, wouldn't she? Did Bethany see something more in him than she had with anyone else? Or was he being pushed away too? Nate swallowed and looked down at his empty mug.

Donna reached across the table to touch his arm. "I know she likes you, and I'm not just saying that. There's an easiness about her these last few weeks. I can only attribute that to you."

"I think she's backing away."

Donna looked down and shook her head. "Fools," she said under her breath.

They sat in silence for a few seconds. "Your grandmother's estate sale was this morning. How'd it go?"

"There was a good crowd there when I left."

"And the house?"

"Del is accepting bids for another couple of weeks. I'm not sure how fast houses move this time of year, but we're hoping someone likes the minimum bid."

"Marcine was a sweetheart. Such a gifted artist. Her bird figurines were precious."

"That she was." Nate stood. "Well, I'm glad you're doing well. Thanks for the advice. It was pretty enlightening."

Donna stepped up to him for a hug. "You're welcome,"

she said, patting his back as they embraced. "I'll tell her you stopped by." She winked at him as he pulled away.

Nate left through the back door with a stern warning from Donna never to use the front door again. He closed the gate behind him and sat in the Rover before he pulled away from the curb, heading to Marcine's empty house where he could sit in the silence and gather his thoughts about what to do next.

Chapter Nineteen

L ater that day, Bethany stood at the kitchen window and watched her parents' Navigator pull away from the house. Gran left with them.

When Lillian mentioned that Gran would be going back to the Twin Cities with them, Bethany hadn't expected Gran to give in so easily. Donna Marconi liked her routine, enjoyed her alone time. She'd put up a fight, Bethany figured. But when Bethany arrived back home, Gran already had her suitcase packed.

"Gran, can I talk to you?" Bethany had asked when she came into the kitchen where her father sat at the table with his mother. Lillian barged through the back door behind her and stopped, like she finally had Bethany cornered. A fly caught in a spider's web.

In the privacy of the bedroom, Gran spoke in a soothing tone, saying that she thought it a good idea to spend the week with her son and daughter-in-law to "see how the old

folks live in those glorified jails called retirements homes."
Bethany laughed despite the sinking feeling in the pit of her
stomach.

Now, as Bethany watched the car turn onto Little Pine
Road and drive out of sight, she sighed. Bethany turned
away from the window and sat down at the kitchen table,
avoiding Gran's empty chair. She moved through the
motions of eating the salad that she didn't have the heart to
add anything to except a handful of spinach and a few
unwashed cherry tomatoes. After that, she folded her
clothes in the laundry basket, brushed her teeth, and went
to bed even though there was still light on the horizon.

Of course it was another restless night. Up and down,
dreaming, tossing, lying wide-eyed in the dark bedroom,
Bethany's mind was in overdrive. At 4:30 in the morning,
she got up to clean the bathroom. When she finished, the
kitchen cabinets fell victim to her restless energy. She pulled
everything out to wash and rearrange. An old Corelle dinner
set she used in college. Gran's hand-painted platters. Coffee
mugs galore. Even a coffee bean grinder still in the box. It
all ended up on the counters and then spilled into the living
room when Bethany ran out of counter space. She had to get
out of the house.

As the sun peeked over the trees to the east, Bethany
threw on the shin-length parka and her white hat to take an
early morning walk. It might help clear her head. The
stillness of the neighborhood soothed her, and the path
along River Rock Road afforded her a view of the frozen lake
off to the south as she walked. Her boots crunched on the
snow-packed street, keeping rhythm with her breath puffing

out in great clouds of condensation. It was so cold it hurt to breathe. She buried her nose in the folds of her coat.

As Bethany followed the curve, she zeroed in on the area two blocks away where her road intersected with Water Street. Marcine's house sat on the corner, guarded by the imposing white pine that towered over the yard. Nate's Rover was in the drive. She took a deep breath and kept walking in that direction.

With Gran gone, Bethany wondered what her week would look like. She'd never thought about the amount of time she spent eating meals with Gran, doing household chores, and once in a while, shuttling her to an appointment since Gran didn't like driving on icy roads. Their routines and schedules meshed so well together it seemed effortless. But now what?

Bethany's paced slowed as she neared Marcine's house. She could see into the front picture window straight through the living and dining rooms and out to the back patio. Movement in the living room made her heart jump. Nate was up.

She'd had no intention of stopping there when she left the house, but an invisible force compelled Bethany to move forward. As she followed the sidewalk up to the house, matching her footsteps with the larger tracks in the snow, Nate opened the door. Bethany stopped.

They stared at each other for a frozen moment. Bethany couldn't read his expression, but Nate's appearance almost left her breathless. His jaw sported the rough shadow of a beard, accentuating his dark good looks. He stood against the door in a white T-shirt and jeans, one hand stuffed into his pants pocket, the other holding the door open, like a barefooted model for a cologne ad. His silence alarmed her even more when he turned his back and went into the house, opening the door wider in the process so she could come inside. She shut the door behind her. Nate stood in the middle of the room, arms crossed.

Bethany pulled off her hat, fluffed her hair to life.

"I'm not sure why I'm here. Or what I want to say." Her voice croaked from so little use since Gran left.

Nate's brows dipped. Still, he was as quiet as a church bell on Monday.

"Gran went back to Minneapolis with my parents for the week. She might move there."

Nate scratched the back of his neck and looked at the floor.

Bethany took a step closer. "I should have called."

"Yeah?" Nate said in a hushed tone. "Or at least answered one of my calls?"

"I was angry. Confused. Trust me, you don't want to be around me when I'm like that."

"Why don't you let me make that decision?"

Bethany looked away, shaking her head. "My family problems shouldn't be your problem."

He let out a short, humorless laugh. "But they are, Bethany. Don't you see?"

"I'm sorry. I should have—"

"Cut me off sooner? Is that what you're going to say?"

"Stop. Please. I don't need that."

He ran both hands through his hair, making it stick up in spots. "What do you want me to do, Bethany? I keep trying to be here for you, but it's like you don't want me to try. Are we not on the same page?"

"Honestly, I don't know."

Again, the forced smile that made his eyes even more cold. "But I think you do."

She stared at the floor for what seemed like forever, her mind whirling. What had scared her the most over the last few weeks? That she was attracted to Nate, more so to him than any one else she'd dated, but that he wasn't staying? And now with Gran gone, the familiar uncertainty crept in and forced her to confront it once again.

"I need to know that not everyone leaves." Her voice cracked again.

Nate took a step forward. "Not everybody does."

"You will. The house is empty. Someone's going to buy it."

"So what? That doesn't mean we're done."

"You can't live and work in Duluth and then see me on the weekends. It doesn't work that way. Trust me. I—"

"Why don't we try to have a relationship first, and not worry about who's here or there? It's not that hard."

"How would you know? Did you get to see your parents only on weekends?"

"This isn't about parents, Bethany. This is about us."

"Exactly. I can't do long-distance relationships."

"You can't do any relationships."

She shrugged matter-of-factly. "Like I said, everybody leaves."

Bethany couldn't meet his eyes. The indifference from before might still be written on his face, and she'd much prefer to remember his expression full of soulful longing, the way he'd looked at her before this morning. As perfect as Nate was for her, she had to step away. There wasn't any hope that they could carry on a relationship when they were so far apart, and his work would take him even farther away. She'd lose him eventually. Everyone she cared about always left. Her leaving first would make it easier to bear.

Bethany shuffled backward toward the door. "I have to go."

His expression had changed again, those pleading eyes. "Don't. Stay. Let's talk this out."

She shook her head. It was impossible to say what she needed to say. Not when Nate looked at her that way, like he'd do anything for her, whatever she asked. That's why walking away was always the better way. Bethany opened the door, bracing herself again for the brutal cold.

Nate didn't try to stop her.

Chapter Twenty

❧

Nate stopped waiting for Bethany's name to pop up on his phone by midweek. He hadn't heard from her since she walked out of his house early Sunday morning, and he hadn't expected her to call, but against all reason, he hoped Bethany wouldn't end their relationship without a word. He hoped she'd give him the courtesy of a proper send-off if their relationship was over, that she cared enough for him to not pretend it didn't happen. If anything, Nate worried about her being alone too. As a permanent fixture in Bethany's life, Donna's absence was a gaping wound. That had to be hard on Bethany. But most of all, he just missed talking to her.

When he'd gone into work Monday morning, his editor gave him a slew of small pieces to work on, and with the *Coast* feature to pull together in his spare time, his mind stayed occupied. Still, Bethany managed to worm her way into his thoughts at random times during the week. Fleeting reminders of their time together came with the scent of perfume as he walked to the office, the sparrows darting outside his window, and the frost he scraped from his windshield in the early hours of the morning. Even a half-used jar of pasta sauce in his refrigerator brought back memories of the night in the kitchen with Bethany and Jana.

Bethany made it perfectly clear that working through Gran's absence and her aversion to commitments was her burden to bear, yet during the short time they'd reconnected, she'd made an indelible mark on his life. Turning off his feelings like a switch was impossible. And what did it mean for the Gala on Saturday? Did she still want to go? He got his answer on Friday morning.

His phone vibrated in his coat's hip pocket as he stood at the corner of Clements and Washington, waiting for the "walk" light to flash. Rush-hour traffic inched by between him and the three-story Herald building. He fished the phone out and looked at the name on the screen.

Bethany. Finally.

He cleared his throat. "Hello?"

"Hi, Nate." The gravel-laden voice on the other end didn't sound at all like Bethany. *Uh-oh.*

"What's wrong with your voice?"

"I came down with something last night. Fever. Sore throat. Feel like death."

Nate knew what that meant. "Sorry to hear that." He waited.

"Yeah. How are you?"

"Busy. Heading in to work." The "walk" light came on. He stepped off the curb.

"I won't keep you then. Listen—"

Nate didn't want to go there yet. "Have you heard from Gran?

"Nope. Must be enjoying herself." Her tone was flat.

"So what have you been doing to keep busy?" He slowed after he crossed the street. Nate didn't want everyone in the office to listen in on his conversation, so he jogged up the steps of the newspaper building and stopped inside the foyer, resting against the old silver radiator that still put out a decent amount of heat.

Bethany was silent for a few seconds. "Teaching. Helping Darcy with—" Her voice trailed off, then she coughed. He heard the faint sound of classical music in the background. She must be at the studio. *Not so sick after all.*

"Nate, I don't think I'm up for going to the gala. This is the sickest I've been in a long time."

A sarcastic reply came to mind but he swallowed the words and opted for a more understanding one instead. "You don't think you'll feel better by tomorrow?"

"When I get sick, I'm usually down for a while. Sorry."

Even with a voice like a rusty hinge, he loved the sound of it. But she didn't sound very sorry.

"Okay. Well. That's too bad."

"Yeah." More coughing. "So that'll save you a trip back to Hendricks at least."

"I'm coming anyway. Got a few things to wrap up at the house before the auction next week."

"Oh."

He paused. "Maybe I'll stop by, bring you some sickbed necessities. Soup, tissues, a copy of *People*."

"No, better not. Then you'll get sick."

"I can risk it, Bethany. That's what people do who care—"

Another coughing fit interrupted him. He waited until she was finished.

"So maybe I'll see you." He heard the music switch off.

"Maybe," she said. Then, "I'd better go."

What was her hurry?

"Get some rest."

She hung up without another word.

IT WAS A FEW MINUTES BEFORE NATE PLANNED TO leave the office and head toward Hendricks when he got a call from a number he didn't recognize.

Tentatively, he answered.

"Nate? This is Darcy Conti, Bethany's friend."

"Yes. Hello." A thread of alarm wound itself around his throat. Had something happened to Bethany?

"Bethany said she's not able to come to the gala tomorrow night."

"Oh?"

"She's lost her voice so she wanted me to call."

"Sorry to hear that." Should he visit her? Bring her some soup after all?

"Bethany insisted that I give you the tickets to use anyway," Darcy said, pausing.

"I don't know about that. I really don't want to go alone."

"She thought you might feel like that. This seems a little

weird, but she suggested maybe since you know Paige Goff, you two could go together. She's staying at the inn again, and frankly, I feel a little responsible for her."

"Go with Paige Goff? I thought she was finished in town?" Bethany had already lined him up with someone else. Man, she really was an expert at moving on.

Darcy laughed. "She was, but I invited her to the Gala. And since you two have publishing ties in common, I thought you two might be any easy fit. Don't think I'm above using people to my advantage." She laughed again, an impish sound that reminded Nate of wind chimes. "Paige's work will bring a ton of publicity to the inn, so I figured the gala would be another window into Hendricks for her assignment."

Nate didn't want to go with Paige Goff. He couldn't think of a worse fate than Paige trailing after him in place of Bethany. Maybe dangling from a rope tied around his ankles over a pit of hungry hyenas? Nah, that paled in comparison. But he liked Darcy and didn't want to turn her down.

"Of course I'll go with Paige. Looking forward to it." He gritted his teeth.

On the bright side, maybe Darcy would put in a good word for him when she next talked to Bethany. Who was he kidding? He shook his head, drawing a strange look from James across the aisle. Did agreeing to go with an obnoxious woman to score points with Bethany count as desperate? Nate didn't want to think too hard about the answer to that question.

Chapter Twenty-One

❧

One more day.

Bethany closed the gate behind her and lifted the gym bag over her shoulder, wincing with the effort. Somehow she'd developed a kink in her neck during the night. Two sessions that morning, a Mom & Me hour, and vinyasa, hadn't done anything to relieve it. Bethany headed for her house, but then changed directions on the back sidewalk and decided to grab Gran's heating pad.

One more day.

Gran would be back from the Twin Cities tomorrow sometime. Bethany figured there would be orders from her parents, disguised as discussions, when they dropped her off too. Mother's skill at making a person feel empowered while directing the course of her will was legendary. Bethany was positive they'd talked Gran into agreeing to the move. How soon it would happen was Bethany's concern.

She let herself into the mudroom and unlocked the door leading into the kitchen.

"It's about time you wandered home." Gran stood on a chair in front of the kitchen cabinets. Several doors were wide open. "What happened here? I can't find anything I'm looking for."

Bethany dumped her bag on the floor and walked over to give Gran a hug when the older woman stepped off the chair.

"What are you doing home? I wasn't expecting you until tomorrow."

Gran's shoulders slumped with exaggerated agony. "I couldn't stand it one minute longer." She put her hands on her hips, speaking with a mocking air. "'You can do this, but you can't do that. We know what's best of you. You're not capable of making these decisions.'"

"Oh, Gran." Bethany laughed. "I can't even imagine."

"I can't believe I went along with it last Sunday. Why didn't you save me?"

Bethany opened her mouth incredulously. "You're blaming me? I've long since learned you don't do anything you don't want to do."

Gran's wry smile wavered. "Are you sick? Your voice sounds scratchy."

"Just a little sore throat. Not a big deal."

"That's good. Can't have you missing your big date tonight. That's another reason why I wanted to come back early. I wanted to see you in that new dress."

Bethany flushed. "Well, there's been a change of plans."

Gran's chin tilted down and she frowned. "Don't tell me."

"It wouldn't have worked—"

"Bethany!"

"Nate sensed it was coming anyway."

"Of course he did. You're an expert at dropping those not-so-subtle hints."

Bethany collapsed in one of the chairs. "It wasn't like that. I really liked him. A lot."

Gran shook her head, looking at the ceiling. "Then why on earth don't you want to see him anymore?"

Bethany looked at her hands, folded in her lap, and picked at her nail polish. "We agreed that long-distance relationships don't work."

"'*We* decided?'" Gran pursed her lips. "C'mon, Bethany. Remember who you're talking to."

"Fine. I decided." She slumped against chair. "I did really like him."

"That's the first time I've heard you say that about anyone."

Bethany looked up at her grandmother.

Gran pulled out a chair and sat, facing her. "I joke about dying a lot, and I know you don't like it. But I'm being serious now. Someday I won't be around anymore, and I hate to think that you'll be alone."

Bethany looked down again. She chewed on her lip, nodding.

"Nate's good for you, dear. He cares about you a lot."

Bethany snorted. "You've met him once, Gran."

"Another time too. He was here last week before I left."

Bethany sat upright. "What? Where was I?"

"I think you were tearing up the countryside, doing battle with your mother."

"Why did he come here?" Bethany couldn't believe Gran kept this from her until now.

"Well, I think he was looking for you. But then we sat down together and talked. He was very worried about you. Confused too."

Bethany rubbed the side of her face. "I don't blame him. I was confused myself."

Gran studied her. "It's not too late for tonight, you know. You can still fix this."

"No, I can't. I've already given my tickets back to Darcy. She called Nate yesterday to set him up with someone else."

"That doesn't mean you can't go by yourself and set things straight."

"Didn't you hear me? I said I don't have a ticket."

"If you don't cause the death of me someday," Gran said, her voice trailing off as she crossed the kitchen to pluck two tickets out from underneath a stack of gardening catalogs. "You're lucky I'm a lifetime patron of the Arts Guild. Two complimentary tickets." She slapped them on the table in front of Bethany.

Bethany fingered the tickets, not moving from her chair.

"Don't make me dress you myself and shove you out the door," Gran said gruffly.

Bethany sighed. "It's probably too late to get another date. But all right."

. . .

BETHANY WHEELED INTO THE LOT AT STURGEON Widows Tours, her brakes squealing in protest when she stopped a little too quickly in the nearest parking space. Her wheels hit the curb, causing a mini catastrophe inside her car—her purse flew to the floor, spilled its contents, including her metal thermos filled with water, which emitted the most awful *clang* when it hit the underside of the glove compartment. The lid wasn't on tight either. That explained the gurgling sound on her floorboard. Bethany grabbed the thermos before it completely emptied, sending a thin arc of water onto her lap.

She groaned. "I hope this isn't a sign of how tonight will go."

The lot was full, the cars dark. Ethan wasn't there, but she didn't blame him for not waiting. He probably caught an earlier shuttle to Blueberry Point Lodge since it was way past the time she told him she'd meet him. Luckily his Saturday night was free, so he agreed to be her date.

A short distance away, one of the tour buses waited for last-minute guests, its kitschy fiberglass fish resting on the roof, the exhaust churning. She almost forgot that her own car was running as she scrambled to reload her purse and grab the faux fur wrap she borrowed from Gran, but then the ignition sensor beeped at her, and she shut the engine off too.

It was a harried walk-run across the slick pavement. An image of her splayed out on her back looking up at the stars flashed through Bethany's mind all the way to the bus. Wouldn't an ambulance call be a fine way to end the night before it began?

"Cinderella, so glad you made it."

One of Fred Behar's boys sat slumped in the driver's seat, hands thrown over the steering wheel, smirking at her as she hiked her dress up to her knees to avoid ripping the hem. She didn't care that she lacked ladylike decorum at the moment. She was missing the party. What she did care about was the way the kid ogled her as her wrap fell off her shoulders. Bethany bet he wasn't even a month past sixteen years if he was that old.

"Haha. Very funny," she said, snapping her fingers in his ear on the way past to find a seat. "Just get this sorry excuse for my glass coach moving. I'm late!"

The kid's rigid posture and moon-eyed glances in his overhead mirror suggested she'd whipped him back into shape as he buckled his seatbelt and gripped the gearshift with newfound purpose.

They were on their way within a minute, so Bethany settled into her seat with warm currents of air blasting from the vent at her feet. Silently, she rehearsed what she'd say to Nate. She'd say it had been a 24-hour bug, never had one of those in her life. She'd also say she didn't want to cause problems with last-minute plans since Paige counted on him after all, and—

Those were ridiculous excuses, not credible at all. He'd see right through that nonsense to how flighty she was asking him to the gala, then cancelling, then showing up out of the blue with another guy. What if she owned her insecurities once and for all? Was it too late? Would he want the trouble of trying to reboot their relationship when he lived two hours away? Bethany wasn't sure. They could have established a firm foundation before he moved out of Hendricks and who knows what could have happened between them. If she weren't so skittish, Nate could be *the one*. Wouldn't that thrill Gran? But now they were on shaky ground at best.

Blueberry Point Lodge loomed in the distance, lit up like a Christmas tree, as the bus pulled into the gravel drive. Bethany pressed the spot on her chest where her heart threatened to burst through; it beat so hard. She leaned back in her seat to focus on her breathing, closing her eyes and counting until the bus stopped under the porte-cochére. She'd never convince Nate that she was capable of having a mature relationship if she stumbled over her words and shook like gelatin when she finally faced him.

"Have a good night," the Behar boy said as Bethany bounded down the steps.

"Thanks. Plan to," she said over her shoulder. She pushed any doubt away and squared her shoulders as she adjusted the wrap.

As late as she was, a crowd still mingled inside the oak double doors. Bethany made her way up the stone steps, waiting for the line to disperse so she could talk with Sean, who looked uncomfortable yet ruggedly handsome in all black with an open-collared shirt and a red rose pinned to the front of his jacket. Behind him, Darcy dazzled in a red floor-length sheath.

Sean gave her a sweeping look from head to toe when Bethany stepped ahead. "Who are you trying to impress tonight?" When he winked at her, Bethany almost laughed. She was used to him acting a little more reserved.

"If I told you, you'd give away my game plan."

He kissed her cheek. "If I took offense every time you insulted me, you'd have sunk my self-esteem long ago."

"If I didn't bring your colossal-sized ego back down to earth once in a while, you'd be on the moon." Bethany tapped him lightly against the arm before she moved on to Darcy.

Bethany gave Darcy a quick hug and scanned the double room. The ceilings were draped in red and gold gossamer, illuminated by the twin crystal chandeliers overhead, and dozens of diminutive arrangements of tea lights, silk greenery, and delicate red flowers made from handblown glass decorated every surface.

"The room is stunning."

Darcy slumped. "It took two days and about fifty packs of Velcro strips to hang the lights and gossamer."

"I could have helped."

Darcy glanced sideways at Sean. "He insisted on doing it himself. Well, with Matt. Some kind of brotherly deal they had going." Darcy leaned in close, clutching Bethany's arm. "I'm confused," Darcy said in a low voice. "You said you weren't coming. That's why I arranged for Paige to go with Nate."

"You know me. I can't stick to commitments very well."

Darcy laid a hand on Bethany's arm. "If you haven't noticed already, he's over there by the patio doors, looking miserable. Paige has been hovering over him like they're an item."

Bethany looked across the room to the large bank of windows and the French doors that opened onto the stone patio, normally offering a breathtaking view of the lake. At night, the silk drapes were drawn, so coupled with his height, which was always an easy marker, Nate stood out against the yellow backdrop in a wine-hued coat. Even from a distance Bethany marveled at his presence. What did she expect? He turned heads wherever he went, whether wearing a parka and hiking boots or the impeccably tailored jacket he wore now. What she didn't bargain for, however, was the expression he wore, seemingly directed at her. His anger torched Bethany across the room. Nate must have seen her arrive.

"Now I'm not so sure this was a good idea," she mumbled.

Darcy huffed. "Sure it was. Listen, I'll find you in a little bit after everyone gets here." Darcy hugged her. "Don't worry. Everything will work out."

Bethany drifted away, wondering if she should talk with Nate right away or find Ethan and collect her thoughts. Her decision was made for her when Ethan surprised her from behind.

"Late as usual," he said, handing her a steaming glass of dark liquid with a froth of whipped cream on the top.

"I prefer to call it a dramatic entrance." She took a sip. "Delicious. I taste cinnamon, coffee, and something with a little kick. What is this?"

"They're calling it a Kiss of Fire." Ethan cocked an eyebrow. "Does it compare?"

"To all the fiery kisses I've experienced?" She inadvertently glanced in Nate's direction before she caught herself. "This is much better." *Liar.*

Ethan leaned closer and whispered, "Have you spotted him yet?"

Bethany looked around the room then back at Ethan. "Who?"

He laughed. "Why are you even pretending not to know who I'm talking about?"

Bethany cracked a smile. "You're right. And yes, I did spot him."

"Shall I go drag him over here?"

She gripped his arm. "If you even talk to him on my behalf, I'll never bring you another latte."

Ethan took a step back, studying her. "He'll make his way over here eventually. You look fantastic."

"Have I thanked you for coming with me yet? If not, I really appreciate this." Bethany gave him once-over too. "And you clean up nicely yourself."

He puffed out his chest. "If there were any single ladies here who were under seventy, I might use that to my advantage."

Bethany took another sip of the drink. When she glanced in Nate's direction again, she caught him staring her way. The frown was gone. In its place was a look of such intensity that it made the hair stand up on Bethany's arms. She bet Nate was curious about Ethan. Or maybe he wanted to confront her about the obvious change of plans. Either way, Bethany knew the next few hours would define the future for her and Nate.

Chapter Twenty-Two

Nate was almost ready to raid the buffet table to get away from Paige's incessant chatter when Bethany appeared in the foyer. He did a double take, not sure if he'd just conjured up her image because she'd been on his mind so much. But then Sean Stetman kissed Bethany on the cheek, and he was certain he didn't imagine *that*. Why on earth was she here? She'd made the biggest production about being so deathly sick the day before. Obviously a lie.

"I'll be back in a bit," he told Paige, though he doubted she'd mind. Paige turned to Letta Arbuckle and continued the conversation without missing a beat.

Bethany squirmed as Nate approached. One second she hugged her arms across her chest, and the next she clasped her hands together, fidgeting with her bracelet. She glanced around the room as if she wanted to be anywhere but under his scrutiny, but then lifted her chin defensively when Nate stopped in front of her.

She scratched a spot behind her ear. "Hi?"

"I thought you weren't feeling well? Why are you here?"

Bethany frowned and glanced around the room again. She didn't appear too eager to look him in the eye. "I'm feeling much better," she said simply.

"A miraculous recovery."

"I'm lucky like that. Whenever I come down with—"

His frustration boiled over. "Was it just a ploy to blow me off? Honestly, Bethany. If you didn't want me as your date, you could have just said so. Especially after last weekend, I half expected that we wouldn't be coming together anyway. We're adults, right?"

Bethany took a step back, shock registering on her face. "Can I talk to you in private?" she said through her teeth, looking pointedly beyond his left shoulder.

Nate turned around. Paige had followed him after all. "I thought you were talking with Letta?" he asked Paige. "Can I have a minute, please?"

Paige glanced at him, surprised. Maybe his tone had been a bit brusque.

"Of course," she said, looking from him to Bethany. "I wouldn't have interrupted if I knew it was...personal. I'll get us some drinks."

He waited until Paige was out of earshot before he turned back to Bethany.

"This isn't about me being a child, Nate," Bethany snapped.

She was so beautiful, even when anger flushed her face.

The blush velvet dress she wore clung to her curves. Nate could hardly take his eyes off her, and under her white-hot glare, he softened, afraid that a few misspoken words might spell doom to whatever chance they had at fixing their relationship. But then he remembered how he'd bent over backward for her during the last month, how he'd tiptoed around the times when she pulled away for whatever inconsequential reason, and then last weekend. His annoyance returned in a flash. He couldn't play emotional tug-of-war with her anymore. Bethany had had plenty of chances to work through her self-doubt, especially with him as her personal cheerleader, counselor, whatever. She should have realized by now that he was genuine, that he planned to stick around.

He raised his hands, palms up. "Then what is it?"

Bethany started to say something then closed her mouth. She shook her head instead.

A short impeccably dressed man inserted himself into their conversation.

"Sorry, I was over talking with Emily Stetman. Need anything?" he asked Bethany. When she gave him a swift, short shake of her head, he turned to Nate. "I'm Ethan Day. You must be—"

He was not in the mood to be interrupted or to see someone else catering to Bethany, something he should have been doing that night. He put his hand up to stop the man so he could hear Bethany's explanation. It was rude, but he didn't care at the moment.

"Is this how you broke it off with all of the others?" He paused, waiting for her expression to change, to hint at whether he was way off base or had hit the mark. "Just blow off the last guy? Leave him guessing what happened? You can't have a conversation?"

The Ethan guy's eyes widened as he silently turned around and went in the same direction as he first appeared. Bethany watched him go, her features growing tighter by the second. Did she seriously prefer to bring that guy instead of him?

She looked back at Nate, throwing her hands on her hips. "How could you say that to me?"

"Your actions have been pretty telling. Have you not said more than a few times that you get to a point in a relationship and back away? Why should I think I'm any different now?"

Bethany shook her head, looking at the floor. When she met his eyes again, hers were cold blue darts. "I think we need to cool off for a bit. Maybe have this conversation when we're not so upset."

"I think we're about out of time for conversation. Besides, I'm not confident anything would be resolved."

Her eyes narrowed. "I don't do well with ultimatums," she said with a steely set to her jaw.

"It's not an ultimatum. It's fact. I'm starting the California assignment soon. I leave in two weeks."

At that moment, Paige returned, drinks in hand, and overheard Nate. She handed him a wineglass. She had no way of knowing he'd never touched the stuff.

"And it will be amazing to work together," she said, putting a hand on Nate's arm but talking to Bethany. "Did he tell you that we'll be doing a photo feature together? It's for *Coast Magazine*, a huge step up for him—"

Nate leaned away to escape her hand. "What? How did you get involved with it?"

Paige's eyes lit up. "I told you I used to date someone there. He asked me if I had photos to go along with the article."

Nate stuffed his hand in his pants pocket. "Perfect."

He didn't try to hide the dry tone of his voice. It didn't thrill him that Paige seemed to be showing him up, like he was a fledging writer clamoring for bylines, let alone in front of Bethany.

He glanced at Paige again. "I really don't want to discuss business right now." A slight twinge of guilt softened his tone at the end, but the effect on Paige was the same as if he'd barked at her. Paige visibly shrank.

She waved her hand casually. "You're right. Tonight's not the night for anything but love, right?" Her sarcasm was as thick as crystallized honey. "And obviously you two can't keep your hands off each other."

Bethany's eyes bugged out at Paige's snide remark. "I don't have time for this," she said and walked away. A second later, she whirled around and came back. "I do want to make one thing clear."

Nate squared his shoulders. Funny, he thought Bethany had made everything perfectly clear. "I'm all ears."

"You were the one that pursued me. I never said I wanted a relationship. I never led you on." With that, she cut through the crowd and disappeared.

Nate fought the urge to follow her, not wanting to make

a grand public spectacle, at a Valentine's Day event no less. Her decision to come tonight made no sense. She regretted asking him to come, realizing she'd be breaking it off with him soon. That was a given. And Bethany showing up with another man proved his point. Why he ever thought Bethany Marconi would fall for him showed that the dynamics of their relationship hadn't changed much since she embarrassed him in front of their third-grade class.

Chapter Twenty-Three

Last night had been a complete bust.

Bethany blew out the candle in the middle of her kitchen table after she paid the last of her bills and pushed back her chair. She glanced at the coat tree near the front door. Again. The fur wrap clung to a hook, a forlorn reminder of the gala.

But what had she expected? She'd spent the last month dropping hints and not-so-subtle reminders about how she avoided commitments. If there was an inkling that she hadn't pushed him too far away, she'd ask forgiveness and for a second—third? fourth?—chance. But his last words cut through to her heart. They also left no doubt he'd had enough. He'd simply said, "I'm done." Then he walked out of the gala.

Bethany bent over to slip her boots onto her feet. She glanced at her phone for the time. Church service started in twenty minutes. She and Gran needed to head out.

Bits of conversation between her and Nate floated in and out of her memory while she moved through her morning routine. Accusations. Denials. An ongoing dialogue that punctuated the night like needles on skin. When their heated words grew too hot to bear, one or the other retreated, only to end up together again in another corner of the room to pick up where they left off. By the time the string quartet took their break halfway through the party, Bethany was emotionally drained. Nate appeared weary as well, the furrowed lines at the corners of his mouth drawn like a marionette.

Gran came out the back door and down the steps, so Bethany slipped on her coat. When she didn't find her gloves in her coat pockets, she looked under the pillows on her futon and the clothes draped over the armchair. She searched through the closet and in the laundry hamper in the corner of her bathroom. Maybe she'd left them in her car. She'd look there.

She grabbed her wallet and reached for the doorknob.

And stopped.

Something caught her eye on the corner shelf next to the door, the shelf where she kept Gran's pottery pieces and the tiny ceramic sculpture of the flicker that Gran gave Bethany when she was young.

Except now there were two birds.

Bethany stepped closer, her heart thudding underneath all of her layers. Gingerly, she picked up the imposter bird as if it might fly away by a sudden movement and examined it. It was a flicker too. She'd never before made the connection, but now that they sat side by side, she recognized the markings. Of course it was a flicker! Hers, clearly the female, sported the orange shading over its head and the muted colors on her body. The new sculpture was the male with its telltale red flash on top and a more vibrant display of spots. Bethany's mouth went dry. A dizzying array of emotions churned inside of her, so much so that she steadied herself against the door frame.

His and hers.

When had he brought the bird? When he came to see Gran? At some point before that? She'd been so heartless, turning him away when he wanted to help her. And now Nate was heading back to Duluth, if he wasn't on the road already. For home. For good. Even if she wanted to keep their relationship going, it would be impossible now with the way she'd treated him. Distance wasn't an obstacle for a couple on solid ground, but she and Nate never had a chance at that. She didn't allow it. What an idiot she was.

She could at least say goodbye and end their relationship —or what was left of it—on a neutral note. And she should take him the birds, both of them. They were his grandmother's work after all. He should have the pair.

Bethany took them off her shelf, wrapped each one in a cloth napkin and tucked them into her bag. Maybe he hadn't left the house yet. Maybe he was still there loading boxes into the truck. He and Jana had spent the weekend cleaning, at least that was what Jana told her when they ran into each other at D & G Foods on Friday night. Suddenly, Bethany needed to see Nate one last time, to say how sorry she was for her behavior. It might be the last time they saw each other.

She dropped Gran off at church first. It wasn't a two-minute drive between First United Lutheran and the house on Water Street, but to Bethany if felt like a year. The bright yellow auction sign in Marcine's front yard beckoned Bethany with its painful finality.

Good, the truck still sat in the drive. Nate's Rover was parked alongside the street, as well as Jana's dark blue sedan. Bethany pulled in next to the truck and grabbed her bag.

As she hurried past the moving truck with its lift gate open, two men struggled inside with a double-wide bookshelf. The unwieldy piece of furniture banged against the metal sides of the truck as it slipped from one of the men's grasp.

She slowed down on her way to the front door. "Nate's inside?"

The older man, bearing a striking resemblance to Nate, nodded. "Yes, ma'am."

Bethany hitched her bag onto her shoulder as she made her way along the sidewalk. "Thank you," she called over her shoulder.

Taking the porch steps two at a time, she stopped in front of the door.

Should she knock?

The door was barely opened, a crack big enough to peer inside. There was no one in sight, so she pushed on it a bit more. Bethany looked back at the men inside the truck but maneuvering the bookshelf preoccupied them.

"Hello?"

She nudged the door wider and stepped into the foyer.

Her footfalls echoed in the empty room. Well, empty except for an overstuffed gray sofa and a red wingback chair she hadn't noticed before. Music floated down the hallway from the bedrooms, but the low drone of voices seemed to be coming from the kitchen. If Nathan and Jana were talking, she'd excuse herself for interrupting then ask Nate if they could talk privately when he and Jana finished.

Bethany walked through the living room, into the dining room, and stopped.

There was a dining room set in the middle of the room.

A dining room set wasn't the strangest sight she'd ever seen. But she'd watched Nate carry those very chairs into the living room, pushing them into the corner where he stashed the other furniture and boxed knickknacks bound for the estate sale at Del's Auction House two weeks ago. Yet here they were, four ladder-back chairs arranged in perfect symmetry around the oak table. A lit candle filled the room with the scent of a pine forest. And against the wall, the matching hutch. Marcine's bird figurines decorated the shelves once again, another surprise after helping Nate wrap them in newspaper for the trip to Duluth. Slowly, Bethany walked around the table, puzzling at it from all angles as if it might reveal some secrets until she heard someone clear their throat.

"I didn't have the heart to get rid of it. There were a lot of good times around that table."

Nate leaned against the door frame of the kitchen, arms crossed with a lazy smile playing on his lips. A small television on the kitchen counter was on, the source of the voices. Bethany dropped her bag on the table. "I thought you might have left already."

He shook his head. "No," he said simply.

She dug into her bag and brought out the two flicker sculptures. When she unwrapped them, Nate pushed away from the wall and came toward her.

"They look good together, don't they?" Nate took them from her, holding a bird in each palm at eye level. "She really had an eye for details."

Bethany realized she was holding her breath. "Yes, she did."

He gave the birds back to Bethany. "What's up?"

She wavered for a second or two, trying to read his mood. Would he be receptive to what she had to say? Or would he show her the door? Bethany mentally kicked herself. *Stop stalling, Bethany. You've wasted enough time already.*

"I want to apologize."

He stuffed his hands in his pockets, waiting. The animosity he showed so plainly last night was gone now, replaced with a neutral, somewhat winsome look.

"Go on."

She took a deep breath. "I've been thinking about us since I left the gala last night. How I've been going through the motions of having a relationship with you. I'm good at that. I've had a lot of practice."

He shuffled his feet and looked down at them, his brows dipping like he didn't like what he'd heard. But the look was gone when his gaze returned to her.

"But I've come to realize that I don't want to push you

out of my head and pretend that we didn't happen. You were...You are too important to me."

If he wasn't looking at her like that, his brown velvet eyes boring into her like what she said made all the difference in the world, she could say goodbye and leave. But his expression compelled her to stay put.

"So what are you saying?"

She swallowed once, then again. Could she say it? Bethany rubbed the spot on her neck where her pulse fluttered like a hummingbird's wings. So much to lose if she didn't.

"I'm wondering if it's too late."

"Too late for what?" He stood so still.

"I want to try, Nate. Even if it means you're in Duluth and I'm here and we only get to see each other once a month." The words came out in a rush. She couldn't stop them now if she tried. "I've been too afraid to think about seeing one person indefinitely. And no one's been worth it until now. Until you."

Nate stepped forward and took her in his arms. They stood that way, clinging to each other, until his mouth moved against her hair.

"Of course it's not too late, Bethany," he whispered.

She hugged him tighter, breathing in the heady scent of him, feeling his arms pull her closer. Bethany luxuriated in the relief of finally letting her guard down, of trusting someone with the truth about her fears. And even when her self-doubt nearly wrecked her, Bethany knew. Deep down, she knew. Nate wouldn't give up so easily.

Something banged into the front door. Nate and Bethany

jumped apart.

"I thought we were going to have a third set of hands on this thing, Nate!"

One of the men from the truck backed into the living room, struggling with the colossal shelf. On the other end, and still out of sight on the front porch, the other guy grunted. His end dropped on the porch, prompting mumbled curses.

"Sorry!" Nate said, rushing to the door. After some careful maneuvering, he helped them pull it into the room. "Didn't think you were ready to bring it in just yet."

"You have more on that truck than you let on." He took a bandanna out of his pants pocket and wiped his brow across gray temples. "I told your mother I'd be back by three."

"I'll be out in a minute."

The older man left, and Nate looked down at her again. "That's my dad. I'll introduce you in a minute. I thought we should finish here."

But Bethany wasn't paying attention to Nate or his dad. She looked at the bookshelf against the wall. She peered around Nate into the kitchen. Opened boxes sat on the counter. There were dishes stacked in one of the opened cabinets.

"Nate?"

"Yes?"

"Why is stuff being moved into the house when the auction sign is still in the yard? And you're still here?"

His wide grin made her heart skip a beat.

"Haven't had a chance to pull it out yet. There were no

bids coming in. Bad time of year to get rid of a house apparently."

She looked again at the unfamiliar red chair. "But that doesn't explain why stuff is being moved back inside. That couch and chair. The bookshelf and dishes. Where did it come from?"

"Duluth."

His words slowly sank in; their meaning unfolded in her head. "You're *moving* here?"

He shrugged. "We'll probably be seeing each other more than once a month."

"But your work. Did you quit?" It was unbelievable. "Why didn't you say something?"

"No, I didn't quit. I'll be working remotely, covering the area between Two Harbors and Grand Portage. Maybe a trip back to Duluth once every two weeks." He looked down at the two flickers she'd set on the table. "I wanted to see if you were willing to try. Though after last night, I pretty much gave up on the idea. But I figured if I were here, you'd at least see how serious I am. I'm here to stay, Bethany."

Bethany chewed on her lip and looked away. She wasn't one of those sentimental types who cried over everything. But there was some moistness creeping toward the corners of her eyes that was hard to ignore. That had happened more than once these last few weeks. She smiled through the glassiness that clouded her vision. As she dabbed at the wetness, she picked up the male and female flicker and replaced the two delicate figurines on the shelf, side by side, back where they belonged.

Together.

Epilogue

꧁꧂

Nate drove along Highway 61, through the first real snow of the season, in the predawn darkness. The snow melted as soon as it hit the warm pavement; the sounds of the wet road underneath his tires lulled him. It had been unusually warm for October in Hendricks until now. Four to six inches predicted, he'd heard, but it wouldn't last long. The leaves were still on most of the trees, their brilliant colors now draped in white.

Beside him, Bethany wore a not-very-convincing pout. She'd dismissed his idea of stopping at the Sage River Trail pavilion to join the small but devoted Hendricks Hiking Club for a coffee-and-donut break before their sunrise hike. He'd tried before to get her to take part in one of their monthly hikes along the North Shore to no avail. This time, he wasn't taking "no" for an answer. When he'd picked up Bethany, Gran was awake too, wearing her quilted robe, shooing Bethany out the door despite her granddaughter's protests.

"Why don't we head to Duluth for the day? Get in a little early Christmas shopping?" Bethany said brightly as he signaled to turn into the small gravel lot at the trailhead. Desperate, Bethany still hadn't given up on changing his plans. He almost missed the turnoff since it was still somewhat dark.

"I told them we'd be coming." He gripped her hand, gave it an encouraging squeeze. "You can't turn down a Debi's donut."

She groaned. "How many times must I emphasize that I'm not a cold-weather girl? I belong on the beach."

"Then how did you end up in one of the coldest parts of the country?"

Bethany didn't answer. Instead, she puzzled at the empty lot. "Why isn't anyone here yet?"

"We must be early."

Nate didn't wait for another protest, unbuckling his belt to get out of the car. He glanced down the trail to where the pavilion stood fifty feet away. The predawn light and snow disguised it a bit, but he knew it was there. Perfect.

It had been a long road to get to this point as a couple, Nate mused. Once Bethany understood Nate's devotion to making it work between them, her insecurities subsided a little. But it took a solid two months, two *rocky* months, before she accepted the notion that he'd be a constant presence in her life if she allowed it. He let the lease on his Duluth apartment expire and settled into Marcine's house to commute one day a week to Duluth, working the rest of the time remotely from Hendricks.

Nate opened her door.

"Can't we just wait inside the car until they come?" Bethany asked, checking her phone before she stuffed it back in her pocket and got out. She leaned against the Rover, arms crossed. "It's six fifty. Someone should be here by now."

Nate stopped, turned around to face her. "C'mon. We can probably see the sky changing from the pavilion. Let's get there before everyone else."

"It's snowing. There's clouds. No sunrise."

"Maybe we'll get lucky."

They trudged along the trail, listening to dried leaves and acorn shells crunch under their boots. Snow, heavier now, fell in fat flakes all around. The forest was silent except for the *shush* of snow falling through the leaves still clinging to trees.

When they came to the clearing, Bethany stopped. "What's this?"

Light strands hung underneath the pavilion, along the beams, and wrapped around the poles.

"Beautiful, isn't it?" Nate kept his eyes on Bethany, though, who was too busy marveling at the pavilion to notice him smiling.

"Very." Her forehead crinkled. "This is kind of elaborate for a hiking club, don't you think?" She walked under the shelter and sat on top of a picnic table.

Nate stood in front of her, waiting for Bethany to look at him.

When she finally did, she gave him a once-over. "What?"

"I have a little something for you."

"Okay," she said tentatively, her brows pinching together again.

Nate brought the box out of his pocket. A little box of crimson velvet. He held it out to her.

Bethany's eyes widened. Her throat muscles worked above the fur collar of her coat when she took it. He couldn't take his eyes off her.

"Nate," she said in a breathy voice.

He stepped closer. "Now, don't go saying *no* right away. Think about it."

She slowly opened the box. Her eyes widened even more. Then a slow one-sided smile curved her lips.

"Seriously?" she crowed.

Nate fought to keep the smile off his face. "What's wrong with it?"

"It's a *plastic* ring! And if I remember right, the ones you passed out in third grade were much bigger."

Nate rocked back on his heels, pressing a hand to his chest. "I'm offended! Who criticizes the ring after getting a marriage proposal?"

"And it's amethyst. Who proposes with an amethyst ring?"

"What difference does the type of stone make?"

Bethany huffed. "I'm a traditionalist."

He made a show of looking her up and down. From the heeled, fur-trimmed boots that were more cosmopolitan than cold-weather practical to the snowflake-shaped earrings swinging jauntily against her jaw, Bethany looked anything but conventional.

"Really?" he said.

"Really." Her chin jutted out. "Plus, you didn't even *ask* me to marry you."

"I didn't, did I?" Nate shook his head in disappointment. "Pathetic."

Bethany sighed. "I'll say."

"Maybe I should try this again."

Nate pulled an identical box out of his other pocket and dropped to one knee, delighting in the joy of her expression.

"Bethany Marconi, marry me, please."

Bethany hopped off the table. She cupped the box in both hands, holding it close to her chest. As she looked down at the ring, her smile trembled.

"This is real, isn't it?" she asked quietly. Her eyes glistened when she looked up at him.

Nate couldn't help but laugh. "Of course it is."

He took the ring from the box and slipped it onto her outstretched finger. Then he cupped both of his hands around hers. "Of course it is," he said again, not quite believing in the moment. How lucky he was. "No one deserves it more than you."

Bethany smiled. "Yes. Yes, I'll marry you." She tucked her head under his chin, and hugged him. "A million times yes. I love you. So, so much."

Nate wrapped his arms around her, and caught her lips when she looked up at him again, kissing her, tasting the mint-flavored lip balm on her skin. "I love you too."

She pulled away after a minute and looked him in the eye. "There is no hiking club meeting today, is there?"

Pretending to think about it, he looked upward. "Not that I know of."

"So you rigged this all by yourself?"

"I had to use these expensive battery-powered lights again somehow."

"Hmmm." Bethany's grin widened. "Maybe I like cold-weather activities after all. Between ice-fishing shacks and now this."

"See? Good things can happen in places besides the beach." Nate tucked a flyaway strand of hair underneath her hat.

She brushed her lips against his. "Good things happen when we're together."

Are you ready to read LOVE LIKE AIR, Book #3 in the Hearts in Hendricks series?

If you'd like to be a part of a fun-loving group with other bookish friends, helping D.E. Malone name her characters, getting the inside scoop on exclusive giveaways, and talking all things books, please join her Facebook Reader's Group here. We hope you'll join us!

Acknowledgments

I appreciate more than ever the people who contributed to the making of this book. It would not have been possible without you. Many thanks to my trusted, competent readers: Lia London-Gubelin, Pam Humphrey, and Bernadette Walsh-Sukley. Also, thank you to Emily Schieler and Carmen Champion for fielding my questions about certain story elements. I owe much gratitude to Hollie Westring for being Editor Extraordinaire and to Jenny Zemanek for yet another stunning cover. And last but not least, thank you to my family for their love and continuous support.

About the Author

D.E. Malone is the author of the Hearts in Hendricks and Blueberry Point contemporary romance series. She has also written two middle-grade novels, BINGO SUMMER and THE UPSIDE OF DOWN, as Dawn Malone, as well as essays, short stories, and articles for the CHICKEN SOUP FOR THE SOUL series, *Highlights for Children*, the *Wisconsin State Journal*, and other newspapers and magazines. When she's not writing, she can be found reading, biking, and hiking if someone else carries her backpack. She lives in central Illinois. Visit her at www.demalone.com to sign up for her newsletter.

She can also be found on: Facebook, Instagram, Pinterest, and Goodreads @dmalonebooks.

www.ingramcontent.com/pod-product-compliance
Lightning Source LLC
Chambersburg PA
CBHW020607180626
46810CB00007B/2683